SOUL SELECTA

What Reviewers Say About
Gill McKnight's Work

"A departure from the run-of-the-mill lesbian romance, *Goldenseal* is enjoyable for its uniqueness as well as for its plot. This is a story that will engage and characters you will find yourself growing fond of."—*Lambda Literary*

"Gill McKnight has given her readers a delightful romp in *Green Eyed Monster.* The twists and turns of the plot leave the reader turning the pages to see who is the real victim and who is the villain. Along with the roller coaster ride, comes plenty of hot sex to add to the tension. Spending an afternoon with *Green-eyed Monster* is great fun."—*Just About Write*

"Angst, conflict, sex and humor. [*Falling Star*] has all of this and more packed into a tightly written and believable romance. McKnight has penned a sweet and tender romance, balancing the intimacy and sexual tension just right. The conflict is well drawn, and she adds a great dose of humor to make this novel a light and easy read."—*Curve*

In *Green Eyed Monster*…"McKnight succeeds in tantalizing with explosive sex and a bit of bondage; tormenting with sexual frustration and intense longing; tickling your fancy and funny bone; and touching a place where good and evil battle it out. … The plot twists, winning dialogue laced with sarcasm, wit, and charm certainly add to the fun. I recommend this satisfying read for entertainment, fantasy, and sex that stimulate the brain like caffeine."—*Lambda Literary*

Visit us at www.boldstrokesbooks.com

By the Author

Falling Star

Green-eyed Monster

Erosistible

Cool Side of the Pillow

Soul Selecta

The Garoul series:

Goldenseal

Ambereye

Indigo Moon

Silver Collar

SOUL SELECTA

by

Gill McKnight

2015

CREDITS
EDITOR: CINDY CRESAP
PRODUCTION DESIGN: SUSAN RAMUNDO
COVER DESIGN BY SHERI (GRAPHICARTIST2020@HOTMAIL.COM)
COVER ART BY LOUIS MCKNIGHT

Acknowledgments

Much thanks to Jove Bell, Cate Culpepper, and Cindy King for their feedback and critique. I should have listened.

And, as always, to my editor, Cindy Cresap, who makes me listen.

Dedication

For Cate Culpepper.

Prologue

Sappho's Seminary for Artistic Young Ladies, Mitylene 654 BC

"No. She's mine. She was made for me. Can't you see that? Can't you feel it?" Much to her own annoyance, Kleio actually stamped her foot before she could stop herself. Pettiness would undermine rather than reinforce her argument. Her fears were justified by Hathor's disinterested response.

"Calm down, child. Be sensible," the matron said. "It is not up to you or me to decide these things. The Goddess guides our hearts and the Fates move our steps. Now, come sit in the shade and be still."

Hathor made a grab for Kleio's wrist and pulled her onto the stone bench under the lemon tree. Being pressed tight against Hathor's bony hip only made Kleio claustrophobic and overheated. On the crone's other side Eris sat wide-eyed, watching Kleio's tantrum with frightened fascination.

"Stop being so silly," Hathor continued to scold. "You're making a spectacle of yourself before the younger girls." She was referring to Eris who would have been at choral practice but for her septic throat. A quiet and dutiful girl, she had clung to the school matron all day, swallowing her bitter medicines, and now she had an eye-popping front row seat to one of Kleio's patented tragedies. Kleio shot her a spiteful look, and the girl cowed back in her seat.

Kleio lunged to her feet and let her tears flow as violently as she could. "You don't understand," she wailed and moved center stage.

"I understand well enough," Hathor snapped. "Agnethas is going to be married, and there is nothing you, Mistress Sappho, or any of us can do about it."

"I can request an audience with Mistress Sappho," Kleio spoke rapidly, wringing her hands, "and beg her to—"

"Kleio! Stop it now." Hathor's thin, sinewy body thrummed with anger. Even Eris shrank back from her. "This wedding is a political alliance forged years ago by their parents. Do you see Agnethas weeping and wailing like a termagant? No." Hathor did not curb her words. Her anger made the sultry afternoon curdle. "No, you don't. Agnethas has accepted her father's will, as any good daughter should."

"Agnethas is heartbroken," Kleio cried. "She says she will jump into the harbor and drown herself rather than leave the seminary!"

"Nonsense." Hathor was brusque. "The marriage is no more than a treaty. After she has produced an heir, her obligations will be over and she can take you up as her friend again. For goodness sake, be patient. Act like an adult for once." Hathor's patience was stretched to its nonelastic limit. "You youngsters come here from under your nursemaids' skirts petted and spoiled to the point of uselessness. You have no idea of the wider world and what it expects from you. The hormones and hysterics hurtling around this school would dement a harpy." As usual, Hathor began bemoaning her own lot in life until Kleio lost patience. This was her tragedy and her time to tell it.

She stamped her foot again, uncaring that it was silly. Her sandal slapped hard against the stone of the courtyard. "No. I want—"

"Go to your room now!" Hathor roared, pointing to the shady doorway. Eris's mouth rounded into a silent "oh."

Kleio couldn't believe her ears. Sent to her room? The gnarled finger pointed unwaveringly at the door. How could she, Kleio, the most heartbroken in all of Mitylene, be treated so cruelly? No one understood or cared how she felt. Did no one see that her heart had been torn from her and lay bleeding on the floor? Hathor was a dried-up old Spartan cow.

With a wail worthy of a rich man's funeral, she gathered up her skirts and ran into the darkened vestibule where she froze mid flight, her cries dying in her throat. Kleio dropped her toga skirts back to her ankles. Two house slaves were dragging a large wooden box to the main entrance. Agnethas's belongings were being readied for collection. She must be leaving today. Surely it was too soon? They were meant to have several more days together.

Kleio raced to Agnethas's room. She burst into the chamber and ran straight into her arms.

"No. No. No. You said we had more time," she wailed into Agnethas's neck, clinging to her shoulders.

Agnethas pulled back and smiled at her tearstained face. "I was just coming to find you. My father's ship is waiting in the harbor. We sail for Apollonia tonight."

"Apollonia? But that's half a world away."

"No, it isn't, goose. It's right in the middle. And it's where I'm to be married. Pathedros is to be based there for a year, then we move to Alexandria." Her eyes sparkled at this news. "Imagine, me in Alexandria."

Pathedros! Kleio sulked at how easily her rival's name fell from Agnethas's lips. "I'll never see you again," she protested.

"Yes, you will, silly. You know I'll have to come back and visit mother, and of course I'll come see you, too. Now let me kiss your pretty cheeks dry, my sweetest child." Though instead of kissing she brushed Kleio's tears away with her thumb.

Kleio scowled. Child? Already Agnethas spoke like an old matron.

"Please be happy for me, Kleio. You know how much I've longed to get off this island and see the world. And I shall miss you, truly I shall." Agnethas pulled out of their embrace and held Kleio at arm's length, bathing her in a look of compassion.

"You will always be precious to me, my dear little Kleio. Think of me when you sing the songs of love, and remember me when you dance, for I shall be forever in your shadow dancing with you." Her words sounded rehearsed, and Kleio's mood darkened, especially when, with a gentle smile, Agnethas turned away and glided out the door with all the delicacy of movement and dramatic intent three years at the seminary had perfected.

Kleio hid in her room for the rest of the day. Curled up on her bed, she picked her emotions raw, unwilling to let go of her despair though her tears had long since dried and her throat hurt from sobbing. She missed her afternoon classes and deliberately ignored the call for evening meal, determined everyone should notice her misery.

Eventually, the huge villa hushed as twilight gave way to a soft, velvet night. Still, no one approached to see if she needed anything. She knew Hathor was behind it. The old witch was trying to starve her out, trying to make her look foolish in front of the whole school. Well, they could go jump in the Styx for all Kleio cared. The harsh treatment suited her perfectly. The only one she had ever loved, ever needed, was gone. Even now, Agnethas was sailing away from her across the black waters of the Aegean, and no one cared!

A shy tap on the door interrupted her maudlin thoughts. She opened the door a tiny crack to see Eris standing in the hallway with a water pitcher and a plate of flat bread with olives. The child tried to smile, but her intense awkwardness only served to make her lips twitch into a tighter grimace. She opened her mouth to speak, and a dry little squeak rasped from her infected throat. Eris's face scorched with embarrassment. Kleio shook her head sadly and closed the door on her. It was a kind gesture, but Eris had only a walk-on part in this theater. Hathor, or perhaps Mistress Sappho herself, should have been the one to offer comfort, not some stripling girl. Kleio returned to her cot to indulge in more sorrowful reverie.

In the still of night, she finally rose and padded barefoot along the villa's darkened corridors. She was agitated and resentful and uncertain how to proceed in the face of everyone's indifference. How could she face her classmates tomorrow without feeling like a fool? Hathor was to blame for this. Hathor was cruel. Everyone was hateful to her.

Her wandering eventually brought her to the seminary temple. It was an echoing, empty place at night, but by dawn the marble walls would ring with songs of praise for Aphrodite, the school's guardian Goddess. The temple was never left in total darkness. Torches flickered either side of the high stone altar and threw its oblong shadow over Aphrodite's sacred pool. The pool was a natural spring where black volcanic rock formed a cradle for the mystical waters. The hot black stones gave way to the smooth cool marble of the temple floor. Sappho's priestesses scried the thermal waters for portents and gave up prayers to the Goddess of Love.

Kleio gazed into the pewter waters. The pool had not answered her prayers. Why had Agnethas been taken from her leaving her heart in a thousand pieces? How could the Goddess have forsaken such a true and faithful follower? She plucked the fibula from the shoulder of her toga and opened the clasp.

"Oh, Aphrodite, why have you spurned me so? You have allowed my heart to be beaten down until it is no more than dust on a journeyman's road." Her voice echoed high and thin in the dark vaulted ceiling. Its ghostly resonance thrilled her. "I have no joyful voice to sing your praises. My heart takes no pleasure in your dance. I have no hope of seeing again the face of my beloved. My eyes are dimmed, and love is veiled in mourning."

She tore the sharp bronze pin vertically along the vein of her inner forearm and defiantly held her bleeding wrist out over the pool.

"I can no longer suffer the cruelty of love," she cried. "I choose oblivion! Let me be forever remembered as she who gave her soul and love combined, and lost both."

She tore at the vein on her other arm and went deeper than intended. The water rippled as it swallowed her blood. Slightly shocked by her audacity and the sting of her wounds, she sat down clumsily at the edge of the pool. Her wrists throbbed. She was surprised at the heat that came with the pain. She slid down further and lay along the black rock to cool her wrists in the water that was quickly stained coral. Her breathing came hard and fast, peaked by a mild panic. Kleio was stunned at her own brazen actions and watched in awe as the pool drank from her body. The feathery kisses lapping playfully at her wounds mesmerized her. In a short while, she felt tired and hungry, and for the first time that day, cold.

"Drink it all." She watched, fascinated. Would Aphrodite come to her now? "I have no need of this life. Take it and do as you will. For I refuse to exist without love. I refuse to be alone…"

It took five hours for her life to ebb out into the sacred waters.

Eris was the first to find her. The pain in her throat woke her before dawn, and she slipped out to the kitchens for a drink of honey and crushed cloves. She returned with her cup through the temple and saw the pale figure slumped by the pool. Eris immediately understood what she was witnessing. She placed her cup on the edge of the pool and slowly approached the body.

Kleio's face was partially hidden in the crook of her elbow as if she were sleeping. Both her arms trailed out into the wine red water. Eris gently touched a tendril of the dark hair. It ran through her fingers like silk, and she remembered her first day at the seminary, how she had arrived, an overawed and frightened child from the provinces. The inner courtyard had been full of girls of all ages enjoying a break from lessons. And there, in the center of the largest group, stood Kleio, the most popular, talented, and beautiful creature Eris had ever seen. The blue-black flame of her hair danced in the sunlight and her eyes flashed as she spoke. She was vibrant, full of poetry and passion, and when she smiled, she split Eris's heart like a ripened pomegranate.

Eris let her fingertip trace along the chalk white cheek that once was so sun-kissed and achingly out of reach. She pursed her lips and blew the softest of kisses across that coveted cheek. The breath of her kiss moved across to a delicate earlobe and then along a dark eyebrow, as curved as Eros's bow arched over thick, and forever still, eyelashes. Hesitantly, she leaned forward and placed a real kiss on the corner of Kleio's lips. She had always imagined they would be as sweet as honeyed figs. They tasted of tears.

Sorrow crawled through Eris like a nest of newborn spiders. Every crevice, every niche within her where hope or happiness cowered was caught up in webs. She sat beside the body for several heartbeats whispering a prayer and savoring these last precious moments. And as she sat, a great pain grew in her chest. She imagined a space formed in the shape of Kleio laid open like a wound, as if a living part of her had been torn away.

Clatter came from the kitchens. The slaves were beginning their morning chores. Only then did Eris raise the alarm and allow the quiet intimacy of the dawn to burn away. Hurried footsteps echoed down the halls. A hard hand fell on her shoulder and pulled her roughly away. Hathor had been summoned.

"Oh, merciful Gods," the matron whispered, gawping at the pale corpse and bloody water. "What sacrilege. What woe! Oh, Kleio, child, what a curse to call upon yourself."

CHAPTER ONE

The Elysian Fields

Sometimes the Gods, and there are many of them, make decisions about our lives long before the people we become… well, become.

For instance, sometimes they designate "soul mates." Soul mates are a spiritual expression of Love in its deepest, purest form, and as such they are fated for replication and reconnection over and over, again and again, throughout all time.

The energy instilled by this devotion is vital to the Gods. It is their manna. Imagine divine battery power pulsing love and harmony out into the universe and contributing to the balance of all things good. Above all, it provides hope for those still looking for that elusive connection, that one true love, that "other half" who completes the shape of the heart. And why not? After all, hope is the only magic, the one true faith.

It's a simple existence for a soul mate, you might think. Not that difficult. Their future has been preordained. All they have to do is sit tight and the love of their life will fall into their lap. Of course, there has to be a right time and place for that perfect moment, the force majeure, the beautiful fall, and bam! It's love and the happy ever after has come home to roost. Sounds simple, doesn't it? Well, believe me it isn't.

I am the Soul Selector and it is *I* who am responsible for those magical little moments. Those oases of romance; the twinkle in an eye, the perfume that enchanted, the pounding heart, dilated pupils, all of that is my work. Mine and mine alone. And I am sick of it.

As the Soul Selector, I have a subtle and complex role in the making of love. I have to identify these soul mates as they come into being, and they can arrive at any point in time across your puny world. Some are returning souls that have been ebbing in and out of existence for millennia. Others are all shiny and new. I tag them at birth and let them run wild, under my watchful eye of course. Over their teeny-weeny lifespans, I nudge them gently toward each other and kindle the romance that pours all that wonderful soul love out into the universe.

Herding horny cats is easier. This is because soul mates are notoriously stupid entities, and that is because their overriding spiritual condition is one of searching. They'll search high and low to be whole. They search for unity. They search for love. They search relentlessly. Remember, they are preconditioned to do this, and this makes them remarkably vague regarding the real world surrounding them.

Other souls, the normal kind, just get on with living. They express their singular free will through an open association with love, passion, heartbreak, and all the rest of the emotional spectrum. They are cyclical. They can fall in and out of love at will. Nothing universal or epic depends on normal souls being happy or sad, unlike soul mates. Soul mates have to be blissed out for anything to get done on the celestial plane. So my job is to glue soul mates together as fast as possible. I have a few tricks up my sleeve like déjà vu, sexual chemistry, and even dreams. I use all of these to subconsciously align my souls. They really are clueless otherwise.

So, to recap: soul mates can get a little distracted, and if you get landed with a couple of shiny new ones, then soul selecting can become a chore. I had the misfortune of getting a pair just like that not long ago. They were brand new unproven souls, and in my defense, lots of things I had no control over went wrong. I know it sounds like I'm making excuses, but believe me, these two were either very charmed or very cursed. Sometimes the line between the two is wafer thin.

CHAPTER TWO

The United States of America

"Jes-see! Jes-see! Jes-see!"

The chanting bounced off the sports auditorium walls and echoed back so that the crowd sounded ten times bigger than it actually was. About a hundred stalwarts had turned up to support the Gregory High School women's volleyball team in the state semi finals.

Jesse Colvin prepared to serve what would hopefully be a head-spinning winner. She popped her dimpled trademark grin, threw the ball into the air, and stretched with fluid confidence into full contact. Wham! Her opponents didn't stand a chance.

"Yes!" Her crow of delight was lost in the howls and foot stomps reverberating around the hall. Jesse and the rest of the Gregory team whooped and hugged and traded high fives. They were through to the next round, and it was all due to their lanky, lucky, charismatic captain.

❖

"You were shit fucking hot out there," Val, the middle blocker, called over.

They were in the locker room and still loudly exuberant.

"Yeah. And I pee lava." Jesse was droll. She was pleased with the win, but already her mind was on the next game.

"That's chlamydia," Val said.

"Hell, I'll have some if it makes me jump that high." Others joined in the joke.

"Yeah. Where can we catch it, Jess?"

"Who you been screwing around with?" The real joke being Jess didn't screw around and everyone knew it.

"You guys have the minds of syphilitic sewer monkeys." Jess threw her sneakers into the back of her locker.

"Better than having the bladder of one."

"Tell us about this sewer monkey you're dating. Is he hot?"

"Lava hot, apparently."

Jesse laughed at the banter as she stripped down. She was a tall girl. Tall enough to make a difference on the volleyball court. Her body was lean and well toned, not only from the volleyball but also the swim team. She was also in the science and the media clubs. She might be a girl jock, but she was a smart girl jock who loved an academic challenge as much as a sporting one. Her friendship pool was large, mainly because she was happy to hang out with the geeks as well as the freaks. Jesse loved to talk to anyone about anything she found interesting.

"Here comes the Barbie battalion," Val muttered as the cheerleading squad began to drift in for their afternoon practice. There was not much love lost between the teams. The high spirits in the locker room deflated a little.

"Oh my God, is that aftershave?" A blonde cheerleader flapped her well-manicured hand before her nose. "It stinks in here."

"I think it's Old Spice?" one of her friends suggested. "My granddaddy used to wear it."

"Better than Eau de Ho," Val snapped back. She never could resist a retort and was always supported by her team.

"Do anabolic steroids have an odor?" Bette Harrison drawled in her easy manner. She dumped her gym bag on the bench directly across from Jesse's locker. Bette was the cheerleader captain. The general consensus among the cheerleaders was that the volleyball team were all hulking lesbians, while most of Jesse's teammates thought that the cheerleaders were sluts. Jesse stayed non-committal. Tussles like this didn't interest her.

"I smell sweaty jockstraps." Lorrie Regallia, Bette's best friend, strode in. "Oh, it's you." She tried to rile Val and took a locker a few doors down from Bette.

"Well, you oughtta know. You've sniffed enough of them." Val rose like a fat trout.

Jesse dumped her gear into her bag and grabbed her swimwear. She was tired at the way the atmosphere tanked the minute Bette and her cronies appeared. Jesse wasn't gay herself, and was unconcerned about the predilection of her teammates, though she had her suspicions. Nevertheless, she hated the way Bette wound everyone up, and Lorrie was a loudmouth who never backed down. But there was no point getting into an argument with either of them. It was what it was.

The conversation between the teams burned out as they all changed and went on their way. Jesse got ready for a quick swim, eager to leave the crap behind her and get in the pool. It was her habit to do a few laps after a game. It stretched out her long muscles and calmed her mind. Tonight she'd need a calm mind. The media club was having its AGM that evening. Jesse was outgoing president, and a small election war was being waged over the vacated seat. The voting would be close with egos and tempers flying high. It was not going to be a fun evening.

She pulled on her swimsuit. Her mind was still on the media club when she happened to glance up; Bette Harrison was watching her slide her swimsuit straps over her shoulders with the oddest look on her face. Jesse quickly checked her front to see what had caught Bette's eye. Nothing that she could see.

When she looked up again, Bette was chatting with Lorrie and ignoring her. Shrugging it off, Jesse moved toward the pool corridor.

"Happy pearl diving out there."

Jesse didn't look back. She knew Lorrie's voice anywhere.

Chapter Three

Hey, Jesse, need a lift?" Marcie Tate called across the parking lot. They had just left the media club meeting, which had seriously overrun with the predicted tantrums Jesse had feared.

"Yeah, can you give me five minutes? I need to get something from my locker." Jesse sprinted toward the auditorium. It opened late in the evenings, but it was nearly closing time and she had to hurry.

"Be quick. It's nearly nine. My mom will flip." Marcie ducked into her car and started the engine.

Jesse had forgotten her swim goggles. Normally, she wouldn't have worried, but she might be lucky and they'd still be there. She'd hate to lose them.

"Great." The goggles still hung from the locker door. She pushed them into her coat pocket and was about to leave when she heard a shower running. Someone was putting in serious overtime.

"Don't bite."

The words brought her up short. They were followed by a deep, throaty chuckle. Jesse strained to listen over the splash of water.

"Put your weight on your left leg. I'll support you." More giggles followed, and then a deep groan that singed Jesse's body like a flame racing along her nerve endings. She knew she'd stumbled across something of a sexual nature. Curious, and urged on by the primitive tug in her belly, Jesse quietly moved toward the shower stalls.

The acoustics became louder with the sound of running water and giggling voices bouncing off every tiled surface. Steam hung from the ceiling in a warm, fuggy blanket, so the hot water must have been running for some time. The voices were coming from the cubicle farthest away from the door. Carefully choosing her line of approach, Jesse managed to peer into the stall while the oblique angle gave her maximum cover from its occupants.

Her breath caught. Bette Harrison and Lorrie Regallia were in there together. Both cheerleaders were successful students, both dated football players, both were very popular with the fast crowd. In fact, they were the fast crowd. They were both absolutely gorgeous, and right now, both were entwined in an extremely slippery caress.

Lorrie was on her knees, her face buried in Bette's crotch. Bette's right leg was hooked over Lorrie's shoulder as she clung with one hand to the top of the shower stall for balance. Her other hand was meshed in Lorrie's wet, dark hair, pulling her closer.

Jesse watched transfixed as Lorrie gorged herself, unsure if she was imagining or actually hearing the sound of her lapping tongue. She could clearly hear the soft moans of Bette swaying above her. Lorrie's hand cradled Bette's hip, aiding her balance, and then it slipped away to caress her thigh. Jesse's eyes widened as Lorrie's fingers began to delve into the crease already filled by her busy tongue.

A primitive groan escaped Bette, turning Jesse's belly pangs into a full on sex ache. The blood fled Jesse's knees and head to simultaneously implode in her groin. She leaned on the tiled wall to keep steady.

Lorrie's fingers began a forceful pump, and Bette's cries became more ragged, her hips jerking convulsively against Lorrie's hand.

"More." Her voice was breathless, rasping.

Lorrie twisted her hand slightly and resumed her plunging action, her mouth never leaving Bette's sex.

She's added another finger. Jesse's mind was whirling. She was overheated and so turned on she had no other focus but the slithering, saturated bodies. The additional finger seemed to be the charm. Bette became frantic, her vocalization louder and more guttural. Jesse had never known such noises could come out of a woman. It was far from the pornographic mewling she'd seen in the movies.

That's the sound of real sex. Fuck, it's so hot. The heat between her legs became a pinching knot. She felt like she would pop. But Bette popped first.

"Gonna…come…" She grunted and ground down hard on Lorrie's fingers. With a low, deep groan, she suddenly stilled. Lorrie changed from plunging to small, sharp twists, her tongue swirling along the length of Bette's sex. She obviously knew how to push her over the edge. Bette gave a long wail, and her whole body spasmed with pleasure. Jesse's skin goose-bumped, and she shivered with emphatic excitement.

"Oh God, that was so good. Come here, baby," Bette panted. She stroked Lorrie's face as she smiled up happily from her supine position. Jesse could see the shine of Bette's sex juices on Lorrie's cheek and chin, and another shiver ran through her.

Bette turned her head and gazed languidly to where Jesse stood. She was shocked by Bette's cool stare and ashamed at being caught. Jesse was confused at her compulsion to spy on them in the first place. She stared guiltily at Bette who looked back slyly amused and knowing. Jesse's face blazed as, shoulder scraping along the wall, she clumsily backed out. When she had retreated far enough, Jesse turned and ran. Lorrie's laughter rang after her, along with Bette's lazy adieu. "Have a lovely evening yourself, Jesse."

Chapter Four

"What's up? You're very quiet," Marcie asked as they drove back to their neighborhood.

"Nothing. Guess I'm just tired."

"Yeah. It was a bit wild in there." Marcie was still huffing over the media election. Her candidate had lost.

"Very crazy night," Jesse murmured. Her thoughts were in a whirl. Visions of soapy thighs and fingers swam uncontrolled through her mind. Her body was flushed and tense, the pulse between her legs throbbed relentlessly, and she was angry she had no control over it. A particularly lascivious flashback of a moaning Bette, head flung back, droplets of water streaming down the tanned column of her throat, drew a groan from Jesse before she realized she'd made a noise.

"You okay?" Marcie looked across at her.

"I'm hungry. Need my dinner," she lied and was relieved when Marcie nodded in agreement.

❖

"You're very quiet," her mother said at dinner.

"I'm just tired."

Jesse rushed her dinner. The Colvin family habit on the weekend was to eat late when everyone was home. They'd sit at the dining table and swap news of everyone's working week. Tonight Jesse was edgy. She was itching to leave the table and had barely bothered with the details of the volleyball game. What she really wanted to do was hit the shower and crash early. She was still affected by what she had seen and mortified that Bette and Lorrie had caught her spying on them.

Maybe they knew all along? The thought hit her like a brick. Her fork froze mid bite, her eyes bugged. *I was set up. They wanted a voyeur.*

"What's wrong with your food?" her father asked.

"Nothing. Something went down…the wrong way, I mean."

"Not surprised with the way you're shoveling it in. You're like a pelican. Take time and chew."

After filling the dishwasher in double quick time, she bounded upstairs to her room two steps at a time. She pulled off her sweats and jumped straight in the shower. The tepid water felt good against her overheated skin. This was the coolest she'd felt since sprinting from the locker room to Marcie's car.

She leaned her hands against the tiles and let the water cascade over her head. Finally, in her private little waterfall, she allowed herself the luxury of replaying it all frame by frame. Her nipples puckered under the flow of water as she remembered the sounds of Bette moaning and the rhythmic slap of Lorrie's fingers. Jesse groaned. She grabbed a towel and dried off roughly then threw on an old T-shirt and fell into bed.

Lying on her back, she looked at the ceiling and allowed her feverish dirty thoughts to crowd in. Slowly, she slid her hand across her breast; her nipples hardened and strained through the thin fabric. She ran her fingers around the prominent point and its encircling little bumps. It hardened fractionally more, which surprised her. She brought her other hand to her other breast and caressed the nipple. It also hardened into a tight point. She thought they couldn't become any harder or ache any more, but her slow stimulation increased both. Her clitoris started to throb in direct response to her nipple play. This was the most active and demanding it had ever been since she had discovered it at age ten. What was going on?

Jesse realized she didn't know very much about her body, at least not sexually. Sport was another matter; she knew all about her body's strength and speed and stamina. But she didn't know what Bette and Lorrie knew about their bodies. Especially what Lorrie knew about Bette's.

Her hand slipped under the covers and rested on her sex. She cupped herself, enjoying the moist heat building in her palm. She had masturbated plenty of times before, but never with such a prolonged buildup of sexual tension in her body. Normally, she was only interested in a short, sharp release that helped her sleep well afterward. This evening, she was actually curious about this area of her body. She was curious about sensation. She wanted to learn something new about herself. She wanted to understand what had drawn out those almost animal noises from Bette. She wanted to know what Lorrie knew.

It began softly. She stroked the folds of her labia, surprised at how much wetness her caress extracted. Soon the soft flesh became hot and engorged, the folds thickening under her slippery fingertips. She closed her eyes and thought of Lorrie's fingers dipping into Bette. She would have been swollen like this before Lorrie pushed her fingers all the way in. And then she had pumped Bette like a piston, in and out, while Bette jerked and swayed over her moaning out instructions and calling Lorrie's name.

Jesse dipped a finger inside her own opening. It went in easily. Slowly, she pushed in another. She had never penetrated herself before. Her breathing became labored. Pressure was building in her belly. She withdrew her fingers and trailed them up to her clitoris and hesitated. What was happening? It had nearly doubled in size. That had never happened before.

Hey, this baby's massive. She began to tentatively stroke it and nearly shot bolt upright at the intensity of her light touch. Her breathing fell into a short, rasping moan. Her hips jerked back and forth, becoming increasingly frantic. This was very different from her usual gentle undulations when self-pleasuring. Rather than settle for a quick release, she tried to pace herself, to experiment, using the mental image of Bette and Lorrie as stimulus.

She stroked the hard nub firmly then softly. She pinched it between thumb and forefinger, rubbed with the flat of her fingers, pressed down hard, and tweaked it with gentle consistency. And then, out of the blue, with no warning whatsoever, her orgasm hit in a rush of white light and chest-crushing palpitations. Her spine melted. It felt as if lava rippled through each vertebra to settle in her groin. She bucked and grunted like a rodeo pony and cried out, "Oooh holy fuck!"

❖

Three thousand miles away, on the west coast of Ireland, in a farmhouse on the edge of Lough Meela, Norrie Maguire unexpectedly let out a high-pitched squeak. The sudden and surprising orgasm microwaved her nerve endings and napalmed her unprepared body into a puddle. She felt as if she'd been hit by a heat-seeking missile, directly in the panty area.

"What was that?" her mother looked startled. They were in the kitchen baking scones for the farmer's market.

"Nothing, Ma." Norrie managed an answer though her voice was a register too high. "Someone just walked over my grave." *Except I've just been cremated!* She puffed a breath over her flushed cheeks still shocked at the blaze in her belly.

Alva Maguire gave her a bemused look. "Your grave is it? More like the flu," her mother said. "It's going around the school, isn't it?"

In the mirror beside the back door, Norrie could see how red her face was. She looked like she had a fever. Her hair was plastered to her forehead, and her eyes glittered brightly.

"I feel fine, Ma. It was just a shiver."

❖

In Soul Selector's opinion, this was soul selecting at its finest. She engineered this. At Jesse's true sexual awakening, her libido had now become bonded with that of Norullah Bernadette Therese Maguire, or Norrie for short. Norrie was Jesse's soul mate, and as they were on separate continents, Soul Selector thought it best to "introduce" them as soon as possible.

This impromptu connection would imbue in them a subconscious awareness of each other at a physical level. Cunning, wasn't it? Basically, she'd tuned them into each other's sexual vibration. It didn't matter that they lived half a world away. When they finally met as mature women, this little shortcut would get them into bed quicker and ultimately save her a lot of work. It was brilliant! Her best idea yet.

Of course, this shared orgasm thing wouldn't happen again. It was just a one-off. A "getting to know you" experiment. Soul Selector was going to make this her trademark. She was rather proud of it. In fact, she intended to patent it.

Chapter Five

I'm off to practice, Ma. Call me if you need any help."
Norrie washed the flour from her hands and headed to
the back parlor where the old family upright stood in the corner.

She sat at the Boyd London piano and stretched her fingers
through her practice scales. The battered old relic released a
couple of throaty notes, and soon the regimented exercises
segued into a melody that had been simmering in her head for
days. Slowly, she reduced it to a richer texture with every passing
minute revealing a little more of the final flavor.

The strange "rush" she'd experienced in the kitchen had
galvanized an elusive chord sequence in her mind. She had
finally found the missing element she was looking for, and now
she had to test it out before it fizzled away. Her nimble fingers
blended in her thoughts and feelings until the sweetest, most
luscious melody began to caramelize on the keyboard. It was
a seductive rhythm that she knew would induce hips to sway
and hearts to swell rather than toes to tap. It had a smooth, sexy
tempo, and she had no idea where it came from except that it had
exploded inside her while she kneaded dough, and now it was
clamoring to get out. She allowed it another dance across the
keyboard before noting it down.

Music was Norrie Maguire's gift in this life. She could
read, write, and play it since she was old enough to blow into a

tin whistle. Music was elasticity in her hands. Though she was only sixteen, her innate ability had taught her how to extend and condense a musical score until it rolled under her fingers like baking dough. Music was energy to her, vibrant and humming, running in patterns along the fine hairs on her arms down into the timbers of the tired old piano. Her music brought the old beast to life. No longer did it skulk forgotten in the corner as it had for generations. Norrie made it hop and roar like a dancing bear, and in her quieter moods, purr like a cream-filled kitten.

Her teenage dream was to make music her career. Norrie wanted to go to America when she was old enough. She wanted to be a professional musician in Nashville, Memphis, New Orleans, Chicago, everywhere, anywhere. Anywhere that music had its roots, she had to be there, work there, see it.

"What's that you're playing, sweetheart?" Her father stopped by the doorway. He was just in from the fields and smelled of pig meal and mud. The achingly seductive notes brought him to a halt. "It sounds very…modern." He groped for the word.

"Just something that came together this morning, Da. Do you like it?" A few more bars led into a very voluptuous bridge, then on to another grindingly sensuous chorus. It definitely had a mature theme.

"As long as there's no lyrics. Okay?" He smiled and tried nodding his head in time. Norrie noticed his unease and stopped playing. She had the song sorted out in her head now and had already begun to notate it. "Where's your mother?" he asked.

"In the kitchen. We've been baking."

"Aha," he said. She watched him make a beeline for the kitchen and slowly stood to follow. There came the click of the kettle and her mother's laugh.

"What?" Her father's deep voice traveled down the hallway.

"Malachy Maguire, I can read you like a holy order," her mother answered. "You're dismayed by that music."

"She's growing up fast, Alva," he admitted. "Almost too fast."

"Sure she'll always be her daddy's girl."

Norrie decided it was time to get into the kitchen before the conversation became completely embarrassing. Her mother dumped a heaped spoon of loose tea into the teapot.

"Just in time for a cuppa, love," she said, and her parents' conversation changed to news from the market and the price of hay.

CHAPTER SIX

Nearly two weeks had passed, and Jesse managed to avoid contact with either Bette or Lorrie. This wasn't easy as she shared French and math classes with Bette and the sports facilities with both. In fact, she was so busy trying to avoid them that she ended up registering their movements more than ever.

She knew when they lunched, where they went at recess, and their study times at the library. The cheerleading timetable was etched on her mind as much as the volleyball and swimming squad schedules. It unnerved her to see them walking side by side from the parking lot on the mornings they shared a ride in. She found out through a third party, Lorrie's mom had the car on Tuesday and Thursdays because she was having an extramarital affair. *That's how sad I am. I even know what Lorrie's mom does with the manager of Topshop.* Jesse was appalled by her obsessive behavior.

She started to use the back entrance and circumnavigate far-flung side corridors, relieved her hall locker was nowhere near either of theirs. It occurred to her that in some macabre way she was fixated on them, and began to stress as to why. Was she really running away to avoid them? Or was she actually spying on them on some hidden agenda she wasn't even aware of? It couldn't be healthy. She was confused and creeped out, and that made her uneasy with herself. And all of it made her irritated with

Bette and Lorrie. Her moodiness, her creepy behavior, it was all their fault. They strolled through corridors, cafeterias, life, as if nothing could ever annoy them. They were some of the prettiest girls in school and had great clothes, cars, and boyfriends; and only Jesse knew they were phonies. To add insult to injury, Bette and Lorrie knew she knew and still they didn't give a rat's ass. It was all a joke to them.

On Wednesday morning, Bette was missing from French class. When Jesse realized this from her seat at the back, she relaxed in a way she hadn't for weeks. She began to enjoy a class she usually excelled in. Recently, the class had become awkward for her due to Bette's presence. It didn't matter that she hadn't so much as looked in her direction. Jesse's eyes burned holes in her back just the same.

Her reprieve ran out almost immediately after the bell rang, and Bette came running down the corridor. A top grade student herself, she was in a hurry to catch up with her school day. She caught Jesse at her hall locker.

"Hi." Bette stopped beside her. "I had a doctor's appointment. Any chance I could borrow your notes?"

"Sure." Jesse tried to look cool while avoiding eye contact. She reached into her locker for the folder.

"Thanks." Bette leaned against the locker next to hers. "I'll get them straight back to you. I can't afford to miss a thing with the midterms coming up."

Unsure of how to be on this first meeting with this weirdly friendlier, lesbian version of Bette, Jesse tossed the file at her without thinking. She was instantly ashamed of her ill mannered gesture. Bette's face stiffened, she heaved the folder back into Jesse's arms.

"Thanks, but I'm sure I can do better elsewhere." She turned and strode away with her head high and her back ramrod straight. Jesse looked after her feeling small and mean, and thoroughly disgusted with herself.

To add to her feeling of shabbiness, Val sidled up to her. "What did you do to get the poodle in such a snit?" Her eyes gleamed with malice.

Jesse shook her head impatiently. "Nothing I'm proud of." With a sigh, she took off down the hall after Bette.

"Bette. Wait up," she called. Bette slowed and allowed Jesse to catch up. "That was an ugly way to act, and I'm sorry. Look, let's have coffee or something. I think we need to talk."

Bette glared at her so coldly Jesse backed up a step.

"Well, at least I do," she mumbled, expecting a barrage of abuse. Bette continued to glare at her for a long moment, and then her gaze defrosted and she relaxed a little.

"Okay," she said, and turned and headed toward the main door with Jesse trotting behind.

They emerged onto the quadrangle and, without a word, strode across campus to the cafeteria. There they grabbed paper cups of disgusting coffee from the vending machine and found a quiet corner.

Jesse took a deep breath and rushed straight in. "Look, I want to apologize for what I did back there. I'm not even sure where that came from, and I'm sorry I said it."

Bette sipped her coffee thoughtfully before responding. "I know where it came from. First of all, you're defensive because of what happened in the showers. You're uncomfortable with what you saw and how you feel about it. Secondly, you're punishing me because you don't know how to deal with those feelings. Well, that's your problem, not mine, so don't dump on me. You know very well where my preference lies. Your behavior was cheap, but I assume you were protecting yourself. So that's where it's coming from. That's what it's about." She took another sip of coffee watching Jesse over the plastic rim.

Jesse bristled. "I see Psychology 101 is going to be your major? And for the record, I've no idea where your preference lies, nor do I care. As far as the school is concerned, you date

Jimmy Maaser. What you do behind his back with Lorrie is your business. Just keep it away from me. I don't give a damn either way," she said emphatically. "And you and Lorrie don't need to worry about the…the shower incident." Here she tried to sound as nonchalant as possible. "I've no intention of mentioning it to anyone."

Bette laughed at her largess. "Honey, there are already so many nasty rumors about my sex life, believe me, a lesbian extravaganza in the showers with Lorrie is old news. Anything, and I mean anything, you could say would just be a drop in the putrid ocean of small town malice. Constant sexploitation is the best camouflage I have. All that scandal, innuendo, and sick humor gives me the freedom to do what I want in my real world. I could get caught red-handed fucking Lorrie on the principal's car hood, and in under an hour, it would be no more believable than any of the other juicy rumors floating about. It probably wouldn't even be the worst one."

Jesse looked blankly at her, uncertain what to say. Bette shrugged and gave a hard, quirky smile. "I'm gay and I'm gorgeous," she stated flatly. "So suck it up."

Jesse had no idea how.

CHAPTER SEVEN

What she did do was call a tenuous truce with Bette and Lorrie and, consequently, capped her own fears and prejudices.

Jesse and Bette started to share study time in the language labs, and once or twice sat together in class. It made sense as the midterm exams were coming up. Each was a serious student, and if they worked together combining their strengths and pooling resources, they were confident they could ace the exams.

The odd looks this new partnership garnered soon melted away. Everyone was focused on midterms, and all sorts of class alliances were being formed and reformed. They were merely one of many temporary study groups.

This newly developed trust began to trickle over into their social sphere. Jesse and Bette's coffee breaks began to include Lorrie. Her humor was as stinging as a hypodermic, and their break times were full of laughter. It surprised Jesse what good company Lorrie could be, but then she was learning lots of new things about these two.

Val had the most difficulty with these changes. Unsure of how to deal with Jesse's new term time allegiance, she withdrew and sulked. Which left Jesse with more freed up social time than she cared for. Val had been one of the crowd she hung out with on weekends, and Jesse expected to miss her a lot more than she actually did. In reality, it was a relief to not have to listen to Val's constant bitching and vacant gossip. Val's silent treatment turned out not to be such a big punishment after all. Determined not to feel lonely or upset, Jesse used the extra time for study.

❖

A week before midterms, Bette arranged to meet Jesse in a downtown bookstore Jesse had never known existed. They both shared a love of books, and Jesse was intrigued to hear of a backstreet bookstore she had never been to before. With nothing but another weekend of study stretching out before her, she was happy to accept the invitation.

Jesse arrived early and, instead of hanging around outside in the cold, made her way to a small second floor coffee station.

"Hey, Jesse. Over here." Bette and Jimmy Maaser waved at her from a small side table. Their feet were surrounded by shopping bags. Jesse squeezed through the busy tables and sat beside them.

"We got here early, too," Jimmy said. He had the cheerful, highly infectious grin of a young man everything in life always goes well for. Jesse had not seen Jimmy since Bette had "come out" to her. Now she could barely meet the poor guy's eye. Life was not as rosy as his apple-cheeked smile intimated, if only the poor schmuck knew it. The deceit was an aspect of Bette's true lifestyle that Jesse did not appreciate. They lived in a conservative town, and Jesse understood the need for self-preservation, but to dupe everyone with a fake boyfriend, especially someone as genuinely nice as Jimmy, was kind of cruel.

"We've been shopping," Bette announced unnecessarily.

"You don't say." Jesse began to relax. Bette's business was not hers; they were study buddies, that was all. She had to stop judging people. And anyway, Jimmy was a big, big boy. He'd survive.

"Shoe shopping," Bette elaborated. She pulled the most impractical footwear imaginable from a shoebox with a huge designer label on the lid. "Adorable, aren't they?"

"If you say so," Jesse said. She noted the price tag and calculated the really nice hockey stick she could buy if she had that heavy a wallet.

Jimmy burst out laughing. "You're such a jock, Jesse. I bet you've just spent the money on a skateboard."

Jesse smiled. "Hockey stick."

"I don't know why you're siding with her," Bette scolded him. "He helped me pick them out." She reached across the table and slapped the back of Jimmy's hand. "It's his only use. Jimmy has excellent shoe taste."

Jesse frowned. She was being told something here, but she couldn't unpick the code. Her eyes flitted from Bette to Jimmy, to their touching hands, and shared smiles, and back again. They were laughing like any young couple enjoying the weekend.

"So." Jimmy spoke directly to her, pulling her out of her observations. "What would you like to drink?" he asked.

"Apple juice would be fine." She fumbled in her jeans pocket for change.

"No, I'll get it." Jimmy shooed her cash away and went to get her drink before she could argue. He was halfway to the counter when it clicked. The gaze of several male patrons followed his burly football player build across the room. She turned to Bette.

"He's not your boyfriend at all, is he?" she said, her voice flat. Bette smiled in that cool way Jesse now recognized meant she felt challenged and was ready for a fight.

"Yes, he is," Bette said. "He's the kind every girl should have, an actual friend. But yeah, we're both gay if that's what you mean."

Jesse stared at her for a moment wondering why she was not more surprised. Then she nodded. It all made sense; Jimmy and Bette using each other as camouflage. It was a game within a game, but she'd rather have it that way than Bette making a fool out of him.

"It's funny," she said, and allowed herself a small smile. "It's so clear now, but before I hadn't a clue."

"Ah." Bette leaned back in her chair. She looked more relaxed. "You've expanded your terms of reference," she said. "Maybe you've even plugged in your gaydar?" Her eyes flashed and she motioned turning a dial. "Bling, bling, bling…"

Jesse laughed. "Only you could have a radar that goes bling instead of bleep."

"It's gaydar not radar. And soon you'll be blinging, too. All over the place."

The conversation was still on Jesse's mind when she stumbled onto the Lesbian and Gay section on the bookstore's top floor. There were at least thirty fiction books mixed in with gender studies. This bookstore was the place where the local intelligentsia could cruise interesting bookshelves, and possibly each other. She felt like she'd uncovered a really cool secret society, and it fired her imagination. Jesse pulled out book after book, reading the back cover blurbs on romances, sci-fi, thrillers, fantasy, and was soon lost to this strange, new world.

She found Jimmy on the ground floor at the Sports section with Bette just across from him checking out language study aids. Jesse looked around surreptitiously before approaching the checkout. She was lining up to pay when Bette's voice came over her shoulder and made her jump.

"I have that one." She indicated the book in Jesse's hand. "It's a classic. If you want I can lend you mine?"

Jesse's ears glowed. She took a deep breath and said in what she hoped was a casual voice, "Thanks, but I think I'll buy it anyway."

Bette moved away to continue browsing. Jesse watched her go, then it was her turn at the cash register. *I'm buying my first lesbian novel. What the hell is going on with me?*

Chapter Eight

The lane to the farmhouse was not much more than the score of tractor tires in dirt. Norrie had to walk on the grass verges to keep her school shoes clean. Over the hedgerow, she could see the sheep, heavy with lamb, grazing in the home field. The pregnant ewes were kept closer to the house near their birthing time so her brothers, Michael and Cathal, could keep an eye on them. The bleating hung plaintively in the air mixing in with the drone of a tractor in a far off field.

Peat smoke drifted from the farmhouse chimney and scratched at her nose. She wanted to get out of the chill and into the kitchen where dinner would be simmering on the stove and her mother would be scolding one or other of her brothers about muddy boots. The late afternoon was fading away. Around her, dusk washed the granite hills and dry stone walls a gentle lavender. In the lowering light, the back fields were a patchwork of soft greens and yellows as the afternoon vibrancy faded to warmer, earthen hues like leaves passing through the seasons.

Her great-grandfather built his house from the same stone as the hills, replacing the crofter's cottage he'd been born in. The house stood sturdy and squat, organic in the landscape, as much a part of the hillside as the elm trees that flanked its eastern side and protected against Atlantic storms. As Norrie came down the lane, a lamp lit the parlor window. The yellow oblong of light brought the house to life as if it had smiled at her. The thought filled her with cheer. It meant so many things. It was a welcome home after a long school day. It meant her mother was bustling through the house warding off the dark. Or her father was back from the fields.

She quickened her pace. The mud splashed her stockings and the cold seeped through the soles of her shoes, but it didn't matter. A homespun ballad had been knotted in her head for days. Now it began to unravel. The notes floating through her thoughts fell into musical order. The song was a conduit to the lore surrounding her. Norrie had grown up with stories of giants and Little People in a land where banshees stole the dying and gold lay under the hills. The dolmens, cairns, and castle ruins that studded the mountains and fields surrounding her resonated in the notes forming in her head. She could see them dancing across the countryside.

Her family and her music were all Norrie knew and needed in her small village life. Unlike other girls her age, she was content with that. Fashion, makeup, and boys did not enthrall her. She had no anxiety for the future or exasperation with the present. Her ambivalence was seen as boring by her school friends. Her perceived lack of imagination, combined with her exceptional musical talent, set Norrie adrift from her peers and their pressure to conform. She couldn't indulge in their tastes, their fads, their music. She felt a certain sadness at her loneliness, at being the odd one out, but on some intuitive level was sure her heart would always be well cared for. Norrie knew she was loved and supported by her family, and beyond that, she dreamed of another waiting for her, her soul mate, her lover of many lifetimes. She could feel it in her bones; she believed in such things. If she believed giants once walked these hills and gold was buried under them then why shouldn't she believe in an everlasting, recurring love?

She knew beyond all doubt that somewhere in the world there was another young woman looking for her. At sixteen, Norrie had already realized her sexual orientation and that her soul mate would doubtless be a woman. Perhaps this woman was already dreaming of her, too? She could be nearby, or maybe a million miles away, but wherever she was she would always be Norrie's for the taking.

CHAPTER NINE

Jesse went to her room, excusing herself from the dinner table early in order to study. Instead, she snuggled down with an anthology of lesbian erotica. Bette had loaned her several lesbian themed novels, and Jesse's understanding of this new subculture was expanding rapidly through its literature. Her appetite was insatiable. She was reading everything she could get her hands on, fiction, nonfiction, history, gender studies, politics, everything. It was as if she had lifted the tissue paper off a layer of chocolates and every flavor was her new favorite and she wanted to taste them all.

She flipped through a few pages, and soon her free hand began the slow slide down her belly. Hot and flushed, she began to self-pleasure, only this time with knowing, practiced fingers.

The discovery of lesbian erotica had been cataclysmic. Her understanding of her own sexuality had gone off tilt; it spun wildly, a gyroscope whirling this way and that. Was she, wasn't she? But she dared not express these feelings, not yet, not even to Bette. Especially not Bette.

❖

Jesse's discovery of lesbian erotica was cataclysmic for Norrie's Home Economics class.

"Norullah Bernadette Therese Maguire! What on earth is wrong with you, girl?" Sister Martha Paul bellowed. Norrie lay stunned on the parquet flooring. She stared up wordlessly at the stainless steel light fittings and a gob of chewing gum stuck to the underside of her school bench. *Disgusting. Who did that?* Then Theresa Daley's face was peering down at her.

"Are you all right, Norrie?" she asked. "You keeled over like a sack of spuds."

Norrie sat up brushing the dust off her school skirt. She was thoroughly embarrassed and, with Theresa's help, staggered to her feet. Her cheeks blazed at the stifled giggling all around her. Norrie was mortified. She had squeaked like a scalded hamster then fallen headlong off her stool.

Halfway through class, she had started heating up like a pressure cooker until she'd simply exploded. She couldn't stop it. Her belly was still in knots and her heart was pounding so hard it hurt her breastbone. *I wonder if it's some sort of miracle? Maybe I've been blessed like that girl at Fátima?*

One glance at Sister Martha Paul told her she was far from blessed. The sweat running between her shoulder blades started to cool unpleasantly. She smoothed her crumpled school skirt with shaking hands and stooped to retrieve the books she'd taken along with her on her rapid descent. Theresa scrabbled around beside her helping to tidy up.

"What in hell's name happened?" she asked, wide-eyed, "I thought ya'd had a feckin' heart attack."

"I sort of fainted or something," Norrie said. *Maybe I've an allergy?*

"Do you need the nurse?" Theresa asked hopefully. "Sure, wouldn't it be great to get out of here and dodge class."

"No, I'm fine. Honest."

"Are ye sure?"

"Yes, I'm fine."

"Ah, come on now," Theresa wheedled her. "You're such a spoilsport."

"I'm not going anywhere near Butcher Brennan. My head can fall off first." Norrie was adamant. She was as terrified of the school nurse as the rest of them.

She hunched under her desk to crawl after a wayward pencil, all the time conscious of the dampness in her underwear. This new evidence of her body's strange behavior distressed her even further. In the name of every saint out there, what was wrong with her?

❖

In soul selecting terms, this was what Soul Selector called a bit of a short circuit. The orgasmic connection between Jesse and Norrie was only meant to happen once. Once was all that was needed. It was unfortunate for them to have a repeat performance. She decided to check out the wiring diagram. It was probably a minor problem a little tweak here and there would resolve. After all, this was a prototype. It was obvious she had done the best she could in the circumstances. No one could blame her. Norrie and Jesse were extraordinarily awkward soul mates.

CHAPTER TEN

Things didn't improve. Soul Selector checked and rechecked but found nothing wrong with the prototype. She tried turning it off and on again. That didn't work. She disconnected it completely, but that didn't disconnect them. The subjects were obviously defective and had ruined her experiment. She couldn't stop the orgasmic connection, and Jesse's reading material didn't help matters. The discovery of lesbian erotica nearly ruined her revision timetable. Fortunately, Jesse had enough self-discipline to save her illicit reading, and its associated activities to the late hours after her schoolwork was done.

Babes in Bondage gave Norrie a hot flash that would do a menopausal woman proud. She gave a wavery cry and dropped the vase she was dusting. The cost came out of her savings.

The Survival Guide to Cunnilingus propelled Norrie into her first wet dream. She woke up with a carnal grunt that could grace a courting pig.

Watching Bette bend over to retrieve a hair tie from the locker room floor gave Jesse such an illicit rush that Norrie walked straight into a lamppost.

Chapter Eleven

W hy are you hanging out with them, Jesse? They're a bunch of fucking freaks." Val slammed her locker door. She was pissed. The midterm exams had come and gone and Jesse hadn't returned to her old gang and her old ways. True, she always turned up for sports practice and hung out afterward with the team just like before. But she knew she was walking a tightrope, trying to keep her school activities and all her new friendships balanced.

"Everybody says they're queer. Even Jimmy Maaser. He's a big faggot. They say he's got a boyfriend over at Trinity."

"What's Jimmy Maaser got to do with anything?" Jesse balled up her gear and flung it into her gym bag. She wanted to leave quickly before any more vile gossip was lobbed her way. She used to think Val was cool. How had she missed her homophobia? Now she realized it had always been there camouflaged in humor and an insatiable addiction to scandal and other people's misery.

"I care when one of my friends is mixed up with them."

"What, like you don't have any gay friends? What about the team? Half of them are gay."

"They're not friends. Okay, so we play together and go for drinks after the game, but I don't think of them as friends."

Jesse was finding this side of Val harder and harder to handle. It had been present in some shape or form for several weeks since she started studying with Bette. To Jesse it felt like she and Val had grown apart and very rapidly. Or perhaps, more likely they had outgrown each other?

"What it means," Val continued her tirade, not noticing Jesse was trying to withdraw from the conversation. "What it means is if Pansy Maaser is a queer then what's up with the girlfriend?" She turned and glared at Jesse. "Don't you get it? Bette Harrison is a front. She's a freakin' fag hag, a beard, or whatever they call it. In fact, there's even a rumor that she's into pussy." Val paused for emphasis. Jesse didn't respond so Val went on regardless. "Don't you see? She's a queer. A lezzie!" She paused to allow this vital information to sink into Jesse's skull.

"And I give a damn because…?" Jesse finished packing her gear.

"Well, don't you think it's ironic they call everyone else names when they're all fags themselves?" Val scowled; the conversation was obviously not going the way she had intended. "You need to be careful, Jesse."

"Why's that?"

"Because people are talking."

"And what are they saying?" Jesse stood up, shouldered her bag, and looked squarely at Val.

"They're saying you're too familiar with her…with them." Val bristled.

"And what exactly does too familiar mean?" Jesse pushed on though she knew where this was going.

"How the fuck do I know! I'm just telling you what I'm hearing. I'm your friend here, Jesse. I'm on your side." Val suddenly deflated and backed down. Jesse regarded her for a moment, studying the mean glint in her eye, before turning for the exit. She was almost loath to turn her back on Val; the menace was palpable.

"Thanks, but I decide who I want to be familiar with."

"Oh for God's sake, Jesse," Val called after her. "Get real. People are saying you're queer, too."

Her words echoed in the empty locker room and followed Jesse into the corridor before the swinging door shut them out.

CHAPTER TWELVE

How can I be queer when I haven't done anything except jerk off over a dirty book? Jesse was angry. Angry with Val, with Bette, and with Lorrie and Jimmy, and anyone else who was hiding behind fear and lies. This was the rumor mill in action. The conjecture machine Bette had warned her about, and now she was caught up in its cogs. It was clear Val was jealous that she was still spending time with Bette now that exams were over. Jesse preferred Bette's company and her mature conversation to hanging at the mall or the burger bar with Val and her gang.

Queer. She tried the word on for fit. It was a label, that's all. But was it her label? Did it give her a sense of identity? Well, no. It didn't. It made her worry what her family would think. It didn't make her feel like she belonged to any other family either, because in truth she didn't belong, not really. She hadn't done the dirty deed. She hadn't kissed a girl or touched a breast or stroked a thigh and…other stuff. *Maybe I'm a theoretical lesbian?*

The thought of being with a girl gave her a thrill. Jesse sighed. She was a million miles from doing what Bette and Lorrie did. Her ears still glowed when she thought of what they did. And she felt a little spike of something other than base arousal. She was jealous. She freely admitted it and had the intelligence to understand it was only normal. Bette had become a close friend, close enough for her to form an attachment. She was her first gay friend.

Through this friendship a glimpse of a possible future had opened up. She had seen a tiny sliver of the bigger picture. A world where she could get out of this claustrophobic town and go to study in a major city. There she would make new friends, and some of them would be like Bette and Lorrie and Jimmy. That was the way it was going to be. She couldn't live small town life forever. Already she felt boxed in.

"Hey, wait up." The shout brought Jesse up short. Had Val followed her?

Lorrie Regallia strolled up.

"Hi, Lorrie." Jesse was truly pleased to see her. She was a great alternative to Val. Lorrie was not as close a friend as Bette. They hung out from time to time because of the social overlap and were always cordial to each other.

"Why are you stomping around with a face like the plague?" Lorrie asked.

"I'm not. I've just finished volleyball practice and I'm heading home."

Lorrie fell into step beside her. "I just got kicked out of the library. Didn't realize how late it was until they came around rapping on the tables."

They walked outside to the campus gates. Lorrie asked again, "So? What's up? I can see something's bugging you."

Jesse shrugged. "Nothing." She struggled to shake off the black mood.

"Uh huh." Lorrie wasn't buying it. "I got my mom's car. Want a ride home?"

Jesse looked over at her. "It's not exactly on your way." Lorrie had a fancy address over on the west side while Jesse's family lived out by the rail station.

"It's up to you. I've got the car and I'm offering."

It took barely a second for Jesse to agree. It was late and it had started to rain, and she was still pissed off over the confrontation with Val. A long walk home did not appeal right now. She could wait for the bus, but it was at least a twenty-minute wait. Val would probably catch the same bus, too, and Jesse couldn't stand any more of her petulant glares.

"Okay," she said, glad of the alternative.

Lorrie's little runaround turned out to be fancier than Jesse's father's car. They slid into the front seats just as the heavens opened and a downpour began. Rain pounded the roof, and they were soon cocooned in a world of window mist and nothing more. It felt intimate and cozy.

"Talk about timing." Lorrie turned on the defroster. The wipers thumped back and forth and the radio kicked out eighties tunes from a retro station. Rain bounced hard against the car hood. "We'll wait it out. There's no way I'm driving in this."

"Does this thing have heated seats?" Jesse wriggled down into the passenger seat. "It's amazing. It's like my spine is melting."

Lorrie grinned. "Good, eh?"

They sat watching blurred figures run across the parking lot. Then Lorrie flicked off the radio and turned to face Jesse. "So, what's eating you?"

Jesse drew a circle on the window. Lorrie looked on impassively, waiting. Jesse made the circle a happy face. Lorrie continued to watch, then said, "Actually, there's more speculation about who is eating you."

That caught Jesse's attention. Her gaze locked with Lorrie's.

"I've had this conversation with Val already," she said.

"Ah." Lorrie nodded knowingly. "It's always a bit of a pisser the first time you get gay bashed by a so-called friend. But you can learn to work the rumors to your advantage."

"And if you can't? Or you don't know how?"

"Then I guess you're out and proud."

Jesse snorted and looked out at the teeming rain. "Out and proud? How can I be outed before I even know if I'm gay? And I'm talking hypothetically here," she said. "Talk about jumping the gun. Some people are so rude."

Lorrie laughed. "Don't sulk. I don't think homophobes have rules, except hate, hate, hate. Just shrug it off. Everyone knows Val's as thick as a cow placenta."

"I did shrug it off. But it's so unfair to be accused when I haven't even kissed…people…" Jesse trailed off. She began to feel uncomfortably hot in the little car.

"I can see how you feel shortchanged."

Jesse slumped further into her deluxe leather seat. Lorrie's own seat squeaked as she shifted her weight. Then she was leaning toward Jesse, lifting her chin with cool, rain-dampened fingers, and covering Jesse's lips with her own. Jesse started, but soon accepted the gentle but insistent sucking on her lips. The soft flesh of their mouths melted into delicious sweetness. A tingle coursed through Jesse, prickling her scalp and thrilling the flesh along her arms and thighs.

As gently as the caress began, Lorrie broke it off. Her gaze was questioning and a rueful smile tugged at her lips. Jesse focused on those lips with more than a little wonder.

"You go get yourself some more of that, honey bun, and I promise things will feel better, no matter what Val or anyone else says."

Jesse could well believe it. She felt a surge of attraction that lasted all of several seconds before her loyalty to Bette quenched it. Lorrie was Bette's girlfriend, and Jesse certainly did not want to be a third wheel. Nevertheless, her first ever same-sex kiss had been exquisite. Wonderful, in fact. And incredibly self-affirming. The queer label sat a little more firmly. She definitely wanted to explore this queerness thing further. Her face must have been a parade of emotions because Lorrie suddenly burst out laughing and dropped a kiss on the tip of her nose.

"Looks like an epiphany to me," she said.

CHAPTER THIRTEEN

Norrie moved from a traditional air to a deeper, more evolved piece that seemed to pulse from her fingertips onto the yellowing keys. The parlor filled with a sublimely sweet tune that held a curious pathos. Her body swayed gently as she poured out a tumult of confusing emotions into the music. The piece stopped as suddenly as it had started. She sat quietly at the piano. A fat tear slid down her cheek.

Her mother looked up from her knitting. Her needles stilled. "That was lovely, pet, but so sad. Is it new?"

"I suppose it is, Ma. It just came out of nowhere." Her back was to her mother so she could surreptitiously wipe away the teardrop. She was as surprised at its appearance as she was with her new tune. A second tear splatted the back of her hand. She didn't understand why she was crying except that she felt sad. A bittersweet yearning had flooded her from nowhere and poured into her music. One moment her fingers were happily dancing through "Toss the Feathers," the next her body felt as brittle as glass. Her mother told her these mood swings and her recent clumsiness were due to the hormones rampaging through her teenage body. Could hormones split her in two and fracture her like a broken chord?

Her mother's hands rested on her lap cupped around her knitting. Aware of her mother's gaze, Norrie composed herself and stood. She didn't want to alarm her mother, but lately she'd been feeling as if something important was slipping away, but she had no idea what. Was this what depression felt like?

"Let's have a cup of tea," she said.

"That would be lovely." Her mother caught at her hand as she passed. "Norrie," she said. "Growing up is hard for a girl, especially one as sensitive as you. You're very gifted, and people can pay dearly for their gifts. Are things all right at school, love? No one's giving you any grief, are they?"

"No, Ma. I'm fine." She wasn't. She was spurned at school. Left to her own devices, making it a long, lonely day. "Sometimes…sometimes I'm thinking of sad songs, that's all." That was the best she could explain it. The sudden void that opened up inside her as if the ground had disappeared from under her, leaving her in free fall with nothing to hold on to. How could she possibly describe that to her mother? To anyone? She went to the kitchen and left her mother counting stitches.

Soul Selector had hoped this wouldn't happen, but over time Norrie became sensitized to Jesse's feelings and life experiences. She was an extremely sensitive girl, and Soul Selector suspected that's what triggered all her moping around. Maybe she'd outgrow it. Teenage moods were unattractive enough without musical accompaniment.

Chapter Fourteen

T he midterms were over so Lorrie threw a party. A toga party. Her parents were away for the weekend and had foolishly entrusted her with the care of their house.

"It's a totally sixties theme," she told Bette and an unenthusiastic Jesse. "We'll be running around drunk dressed in torn up sheets. How crazy is that? Dibs I be Aphrodite."

"What, we have to be gods now?" Bette's initial interest began to wane. "That's fancy dress, not toga."

"Divinity is not compulsory," Lorrie said. "Oh, come on. It'll be fun."

It was the least fun Jesse could think of. She had withdrawn a little from Bette and Lorrie ever since the kiss in the parking lot. It had been a warm, sweet kiss, and as soon as it had started it was over, but it had churned up a morass of emotion for her. She was turning into a panicking prude, unsure of the lusty, forbidden thrills she associated with these two. She'd imprinted on them like an orphaned chick and was embarrassed by her need.

"You'll be surprised at how many people you'll know." Lorrie now turned her persuasive powers on her. "Lots of people." She winked.

"Put me down as a maybe and a maybe not." Jesse refused to be pressed. Lorrie had raised even more reasons to be anxious.

Who would she know at the party? And was Lorrie turning matchmaker?

"You know, you're so freaky it might just work." Bette gave Lorrie a skeptical look and Lorrie beamed.

"So we're on," she said. "It's toga time. Mount Olympus awaits us!"

❖

On party night, Jesse found herself at Lorrie's front door close to midnight with a six-pack, a scowl, and a lot less confidence than when she'd set out. Music blared over the extensive tree-shadowed lawn. Lorrie's home was set back in a wooded lot so far from the nearest neighbors that no one would be disturbed by the raucous laughter and sixties music pouring from the house.

The door was flung open by Jimmy, resplendent in lopsided laurels and toga drapes. He was a very authentic Bacchus with red wine stains all down his front and grapes tucked over his ears.

"Come in, come in, little sis." He bowed and waved her to enter.

"I see you've sucked up as much wine as your toga," she said and crossed the threshold into a wide, airy hallway filled with drunk, half naked teenagers.

"To the left is the dis...de...garmenting room." Jimmy hiccupped his way through his directions. "There you will find a selection of our finest one hundred percent Egyptian cotton bedsheets carefully shredded for your party needs. Oh, and a bowl full off safety pins. Don't forget those." He winked and spun away with an awkward lurch that landed him in the arms of a tall gladiator Jesse recognized from Trinity's basketball team.

Now that's a handsome couple, she mused. Her gaze ran around the hall before she decided to commit. After all, if she was going to hang out in scraps of bed linen with a crowd of strangers, she would need more than a safety pin to feel secure. As she had more or less suspected, same-sex couples were everywhere. Some she even half knew, which was as weird as it was reassuring. This was a gay party. Her first one.

Self-conscious but determined, she headed in the direction Jimmy had pointed and found the dressing room. Stacks of street clothes were for the most part tidily arranged over every available surface. On the bed lay a huge pile of white cotton sheeting ripped into skimpy oblongs. Jesse stripped down and stashed her clothes on top of a dresser. Draping the cloth around her body was a tricky deal. She removed her bra, as the straps were too obvious, though she was keeping her bikini briefs on at all costs. Her toga was a little on the short side, but it was simple enough to pin the folds at her left shoulder and let the drapes fall around her waist and thighs. The hardest thing was actually leaving the room wearing little more than a diaper.

When she came back to the hall, her immediate embarrassment seeped away. The house was full of weirdos dressed exactly like her. In fact, the ensemble gave the same comfort and anonymity of a uniform of sorts. She blended in. Her first gay party and she blended in! *Here I am at a party with a beer bottle in my hand strolling around half naked. And it's cool.*

She cruised the downstairs rooms with growing confidence. The more she looked the more she noted familiar faces. It came as no surprise that these kids, some of them peers, should be laughing and dancing and having fun. It was like any other party she had been to, except this crowd did it in same-sex mode.

"I see the Vestal Virgin has arrived." Lorrie appeared beside her. "Thanks for coming, Jess." Her smile was genuine. "I thought you'd bail."

"I seriously considered it," Jesse confessed. "But I'm glad I made it. This is fun."

Bette came up behind Lorrie and rested her chin on her shoulder, her arms slung casually around Lorrie's waist. Her gaze slid slowly over Jesse's outfit.

"Amo, amas, I love your ass," she drawled. She cracked a sideways grin and Jesse noted the glazed eyes. Bette was stoned. Lorrie, too. She surreptitiously tugged at her toga hemline to make sure her ass was covered.

"Here." Bette handed over a joint.

Jesse shook her head. "Not yet."

She was too self-conscious of her state of dress and overloaded with the sexual tension running through the house. The place was a pheromone farm. The last thing she needed was a further chemical infusion. She felt hot and awkward and wanted to get away and sit by herself for a while.

"Beer." She waved her empty bottle at Bette and Lorrie and scuttled off toward the kitchen. Her body hummed with relief at every step that put her farther from Bette and Lorrie.

❖

Jesse was partway through her third brew when Bette found her perched on the top flight of the stairs. The stairwell had become the chill out zone for party refugees and was hazed in a fog of marijuana smoke.

"So." Bette squeezed in beside her. "How are you enjoying it?" Her speech was less slurred, but she still had a crazy eyed look.

"It's cool. I know at least a dozen people here." Jesse was catching up with her. She'd had a few beers and several tokes and felt incredibly mellow but far from stoned.

"From school?"

"Mostly, and sports fixtures."

"You're looking a little glassy-eyed. Are you smashed, Colvin?" Bette nudged her shoulder.

"A little, but I'm a lightweight compared to you." She became acutely aware of Bette's naked thigh squished against her own. It was electric.

"No. I think you process alcohol quickly. Sign of a fit body. A very fit body." Bette's words hung between them. Jesse caught her gaze and had difficulty reading it. It was intense and dark and a little wild.

"You've been avoiding me lately," Bette said.

Jesse blinked. Bette held her gaze and continued. "Is it because Lorrie kissed you? I'm cool with that, if that's what's bothering you."

Jesse felt her face flame. "It was nothing. Just a friendly peck, is all." She tried a nonchalant shrug but only succeeded in bumping Bette's shoulder more.

"Nothing? A friendly peck?" Bette said. "Oh, wait 'til I tell her. She'll be crushed. She thinks she's your puppy love. Hah!" And she broke into raucous laughter.

"No. No. Nothing like that." It was awful. She felt like a fool. "Don't tell her."

"I told you I was cool," Bette continued. "Lorrie told me the bitches be getting you down." She cocked her head to one side. "She was being supportive, Lorrie-style. Try and look on it in a sisterly hug kind of thing."

Jesse nodded absently. "Yeah, it was sweet of her." And underscored her words for emphasis. "I mean it was nice…for a first kiss. First girl kiss, I mean. I didn't find it sexy or anything. It didn't turn me on." Now her mouth was running on with her and she couldn't stop. She wanted Bette to understand she hadn't hit on Lorrie, or was even thinking about her inappropriately. She'd been too busy thinking about Bette inappropriately to have much time for Lorrie.

Bette laughed. "Lorrie will be devastated."

Jesse smiled weakly and smoothed her forefinger over the condensation beads on her beer bottle. "I'm sure she'll bounce back."

She was conscious of Bette watching her collect the bottle's moisture on her fingertip. She looked lost in thought for a moment. Then she seemed to come to a decision, and she reached for Jesse's hand.

"Come on." They rose to their feet. Neither spoke as Bette led them to a bedroom at the rear of the house.

Jesse went along mute and willing. Her chest felt tight. She knew why she was here. Why she'd followed Bette to the darkened room. They closed the door behind them and stood silently facing each other. Jesse stepped toward Bette and kissed her, and the world ignited.

Their tongues rolled gently, cautiously tasting each other. Jesse began to shiver; she was intoxicated with excitement. She reached for Bette's waist, pulling her closer. Bette fumbled with the pin on her shoulder, and the cloth whispered to the floor soon followed by Bette's own toga. The cool, firm frisson of their naked breasts thrummed at Jesse's body. She trembled in Bette's arms, moaning her need into her mouth.

Bette pulled her to the bed and they tumbled onto the covers. She pressed Jesse onto her back and they lay, legs entwined, kissing until Bette broke the kiss and slithered lower. She pulled Jesse's nipple into her mouth and began to lavish it with long, lazy strokes until Jesse's mind swirled in time with Bette's tongue. Heat built between her legs, and her hips moved in a primal rhythm against Bette's thigh. Bette continued to tease first one breast then the other, massaging with her fingers and then her lips. Her practiced kisses moved from breast to throat to lips while her hands ran over her body thrilling the flesh until she moaned for more. Jesse was sure she was going to explode. The pressure building up in her belly, her chest, and her head was too intense. Her frail human body was going to combust like a firework into a million flaming fragments. Bette began to pull at her briefs, tugging at the cotton waistline and helping Jesse raise her hips to slide them off.

The bedroom door opened a crack, and a shaft of light streaked across the bedroom carpet toward the bed. Jesse froze. Someone slithered into the room. Then the door clicked shut plunging the room back into darkness.

Jesse began to freak, but Bette propped up on her elbow and looked quizzically at their visitor. Their uninvited guest moved quickly toward them. Jesse struggled to sit up, but Bette's hand held her down with the flat of her palm on her chest.

"Relax," she whispered, "it's just Lorrie."

That made Jesse struggle even more, and Bette pressed even firmer. A soft rustle alerted Jesse that Lorrie was shedding her toga. The bed dipped as another body joined them, and she felt the cool touch of Lorrie's skin spooned in behind her. She was lying between Lorrie and Bette. A naked sandwich.

"What have we here?" Lorrie's whisper tickled her ear. "Are you fooling around with my girl, Jesse Colvin? I am shocked. I thought I was your squeeze."

Jesse twisted around to protest. Lorrie took the opportunity to kiss her open mouth, thrusting her tongue in roughly and not at all like their kiss in the parking lot. Bette lowered her head to suck hard on Jesse's nipple. Jesse's cry of shock was lost. Lorrie's kiss was strong and forceful; she devoured Jesse's mouth, sucking hard just as Bette did on her breast.

Lorrie's kiss was totally different from Bette's. She was hard and dominant, pushing Jesse's protestations into whimpers. Meanwhile, Bette gorged herself on Jesse's breasts with renewed energy, nipping the soft swell and flicking the hard tips. Her free hand trailed down Jesse's belly and pushed the panties down past her knees.

Bette's fingers dipped between Jesse's legs playing against the moist curls before separating the outer folds of her sex. Jesse bucked at the intensity of the touch. Lorrie's kiss deepened. She held Jesse tighter, bringing her free hand around Jesse's body to palm a breast, massaging it boldly, rubbing the nipple into an erect peak with the flat of her hand.

Bette's fingertips delicately extracted her sex juices and spread them liberally over her labia. She brushed Jesse's clitoris for a teasing moment, then a solitary finger pushed deep inside her. Jesse bucked against Bette's palm then she felt the warm spasms of her sex tighten around Bette's finger. Bette slid slowly in and out building up a delicate heat that snared Jesse's hips into a matching dance. Sensation thundered through her. She was breathless, out of control, and unable to register all that was happening to her body as it was assaulted on all sides by tongue and touch. Eventually, Bette's fingertips hesitated; she removed her mouth from the breast she was nuzzling and looked up at Jesse with dazed eyes.

"Okay, baby? We gonna do this thing?" she whispered. "We'll make it good for you, Jess. Trust us. Just lay back and let it happen."

Jesse tried to focus on Bette's flushed face nestled against the side of her breast, but Bette's mischievous finger idly circling her pulsing clitoris made it impossible. Lorrie was licking a sensuous trail down her neck, her hand cupping her other breast while her thumb zigzagged over the nipple. Jesse shuddered with pleasure.

Lorrie's hand abandoned her breast and slid down the curve of her back to join Bette's at Jesse's sex. Without hesitation, their fingers co-joined, and in one slow, solid slide, they pushed into her and started to fuck. As one pulled out the other pushed in matching the force of each other's thrusts perfectly. In fluid synchronization, they filled her constantly and persistently in a maddening rhythm. Mouths, teeth, and tongues roamed over her belly, breasts, and buttocks. The relentless penetration quickly pushed Jesse over the edge. She came with a guttural cry that was quickly swallowed by Lorrie's kisses. White light flashed behind her eyelids. The life force seemed to hurtle out of her body and boomerang back, knocking her flat. She arched her back, flung her head back, and howled, "Oh, my Godddd!"

❖

"Oh, my Godddd!"

The congregation of Saint Keelin's froze halfway through the second chorus of "Heart of Jesus Meek and Mild." The organist hit a discordant note as morning mass fell into a startled hush. Even the dust motes seemed to hesitate mid air.

Every head turned toward the Maguire pew, where every member of the Maguire family stared in shock at Norrie who lay prostrated across the prayer stools as supine as the saint herself on the stained glass above.

❖

Well, that was not meant to happen, thought Soul Selector. How embarrassing. Those two were so deeply connected even Soul Selector couldn't break the bond between them. Ironic, considering bonding was what she was aiming for in the first place. *Who knew?* It seemed some soul mates came supplied with their own glue, and these two were glued together so tightly all the light in the universe couldn't squeeze between them. She had to seriously rethink this before the little one imploded.

❖

The following Sunday St. Keelin's offered up special prayers for the Maguire family whose only daughter seemed to be succumbing to Tourette's.

CHAPTER FIFTEEN

O ver here, Jesse."
Jesse looked up from her precariously balanced tray to see Marcie waving from across the cafeteria. It looked like there was a little media club lunch going on. Relieved at the invite, Jesse headed over to Marcie ignoring the snide looks as she passed Val's table.

Val had formed a new posse with the only intention, as far as Jesse could see, of excluding her. She ignored the petty politics. There were several weeks to go to summer break, and she was already discussing colleges with her parents. Her midterm results had been excellent, and she had leverage. She was determined to end up somewhere far away from all this small town shit. All she had to do was work hard, study like crazy, and meet all her commitments for her sports and club activities. Everything else, like Val and her friends, she chose to ignore; life had become complicated enough.

"Hey, guys." She took a seat, aware of dozens of curious eyes burning into her back. The fallout with Val was the current topic for the gossips. She smiled her thanks at this little oasis of media club friendship and ripped open her carton of strawberry milk.

"So," she said, "what's up?" and survived another lunch.

On Mondays, Jesse stayed late to use the pool. Swimming practice was a solitary exercise and allowed her to think while her body stretched through her routine. She was still unsettled at having sex with Bette and Lorrie. A week had passed since the deed, and she was still unsure how she truly felt.

Pop sex they'd called it. It popped up here, it popped up there, and you grabbed at it, just like that. You could take it or leave it. No big deal. She knew they'd laugh at her if they knew the self-inflicted turmoil she put herself through.

When she had left the party, everything had been relaxed between them. All three had cuddled for a few moments, giggling at her riotous climax. They had casually stroked each other's bodies until Lorrie needed to pee and broke the languorous spell. Then they dragged on their togas and went out to mingle with the rest of the party. Jesse stayed ten more minutes before changing into her street clothes and quietly leaving. She needed to find a place where she could sit and process the evening's events. Part of her was smug that her first time was such a mind-bending blast with two hot girls. It filled her with confidence for future adventures. She was eager for more. Yet a part of her was terrified at her own daring. She never thought she could be so reckless, so tempestuous. But one thing she knew for sure, she wanted a girlfriend all her own.

In the swimming pool, her thoughts circled in her head as her body looped the lane. Finally, exhausted both mentally and physically, she exited the water and dressed. A glance at her watch showed a twenty-minute wait for the next bus. *Can I be bothered?* Her feet answered for her. She began the walk home.

Fifteen minutes into her journey, she looked up from her daydreams and saw she was more than halfway home. She was skirting the edge of a rough neighborhood her parents wouldn't be happy with her walking through. Jesse picked up her step.

She was by the thoroughfare that bordered this neighborhood and her own when she saw a dog get hit by a car. It was a young mongrel, and the car drove on, not even slowing down. The dog writhed in the middle of the far lane, its hind leg looked crooked and bloody.

"Shit." Jesse dropped her gym bag and checked the traffic. The next car that came along would kill it if the driver didn't stop, and with the speed these cars made along this stretch of road, she'd be surprised if the driver could even slow down, nevermind stop without causing an accident. If she was fast, she could reach the dog and get it onto the sidewalk before the next wave of traffic arrived. Behind her, she could see the vehicles lined up at the stop light. Any minute now, they would come barreling down and that would be the end of the dog. Measuring the distance to the dog and including the time to scoop it up, *Please don't let it bite,* Jesse reckoned she could make it in time. She made a run for it.

The yelping dog struggled against her chest, and she cursed herself for not considering its weight, but she made it to the far side. In this neighborhood not only were dogs allowed to wander onto dangerous roads, but the safety barriers for the pedestrian area had been ripped out. Jesse stood near the edge breathing hard and checking out the dog. She didn't think the leg was broken though there was a nasty gash that she was sure would need stitches. Maybe she should call her dad to come help? Her cell was in her gym bag on the other side of the road. She hoped no passing opportunist came along and stole it while she stood like a fool on the opposite side. It would be several minutes until the lights turned in her favor again.

She wrapped the dog in her jacket and hunkered down to stroke its brindled head.

"Don't worry, boy. I'll help you. I'll call my dad and everything will be all right. You'll see." She moved to stand up again as a delivery truck roared past. The absent safety rails let the vehicle move too close to the pedestrian area. It also meant Jesse stood too close to the freeway. With only a few inches to spare, the truck's wide, low-slung side mirror clipped the top of her head. Jesse died instantly. She died before her knees had straightened, before she had fully registered the dangerous proximity of the truck. Her last thought on earth was, *How could someone hit a dog and drive on...*

Chapter Sixteen

The Elysian Fields

"What in Hades were you thinking? You just took out one of my people! Talk about friendly fire!" Soul Selector bellowed. "You've snuffed out one half of my soul mates. What am I going to do with point five of a soul mate? I can't have half a soul mate running round. It's unheard of. Have you any idea of the spiritual imbalance, the universal disparity, the cosmic divergence—"

"I'm sorry," Death said. "I'm weally, weally sorry." Soul Selector glared at him. Most people thought Death was all gloom and doom wrapped up in a big black cloak. Well, he wasn't; that was her. Death was a frivolous, fluffy thing. He was all about release and deliverance. He was smiley and sweet as if he'd been stuffed with meringue. He was also slightly rhotacistic, in that he had trouble with his r's. In Soul Selector's opinion, he was also a sloppy worker, which was surprising considering how long he'd been at it.

"I'm not sure what happened." He blinked up at her. "I was in the neighborhood, at a quack house—"

"A quack house?"

"Yes."

"What, like in ducks?"

"No. A QUACK house." He grumped, but she was none the wiser. "Like in dwugs," he said.

"Crack? A crack house? You were on crack?" Soul Selector was horrified. No wonder he'd popped off one of hers. He'd been high as a migrating flamingo.

"No. I was collecting a consignment." He puffed in exasperation, which was totally uncalled for. He was the one being obtuse.

"You're dealing in dwu—drugs?" She tried to make sense of it all. Death on drugs was not a must see.

"Addicts, silly, I was collecting a consignment of addicts," he said. "Dodgy methamphetamine." He winked and tapped his nose. She wanted to slap the meringue clean out of him. "I was collecting several individuals that evening. I turned away for just one minute, and when I looked back, well, there she was, standing beside me, dead."

"That was MY girl. Mine. How could you kill her? How could you miscount? How?" She shouted. It felt good. She needed the release.

Death shrugged. "She must have wandered into my death zone. What can I say? It was a weird night. Those dwug deaths always are. I mean, I was supposed to pick up a dog too, but he was a no-show." Death looked mystified at this. Soul Selector was unsurprised a dog had outsmarted him. "Goodness knows how it happened," he continued, blissfully unaware of the storm cloud brewing over him. "It's not like she was on my list."

"I know…BECAUSE SHE WAS ON MY LIST!"

He held up his hands. "Believe me, I was totally dismayed. It was like I'd seen a ghost. Oops."

"Oh, shut up." Her left eye started to tic, much to her annoyance. It was hard to intimidate Death, or anyone for that matter, when she was inadvertently winking at them. "Can't you put her back before anyone notices?"

Neither of them wanted the Celestial collective to notice the cock up. It could lead to innumerable problems. The Gods didn't like problems unless they'd engineered them themselves.

"Like a zombie?" He looked uncomfortable.

"No. Not like a freakin' zombie. Like a soul mate."

He sighed theatrically. Death loved a good drama so he was sucking this one up. "It's been a whole day in Earth time. She's in the morgue now in a cooler…like a Popsicle, or should I say Popsicgal?" He tittered at his lame joke. "Popsigal, Popsicle. It's a joke, see?"

She glared at him until the inane smile slid off his inane face. Soul Selector had a hard, hot stare she was rather proud of. It was the Greek in her.

"Right, that's it. I'm taking this all the way to the top." This was a bluff, but she had to motivate him into helping her somehow. "You have no right snuffing my people. I'm going to sue!"

"Over my dead body." He came back. Then realizing he'd made another dreadful joke, giggled nervously. Another hard, hot glare soon napalmed that.

"Look, Soulie," he said, trying to placate her. Unfortunately for him, she hated the nickname. "By the time you fill out years and years of paperwork, I'll be collecting the other soul mate. Accept it. You'll have to come up with another plan for these girls. I weally am sorry, and I owe you a lunch. Byeee." With a cute little wave, he faded into a smudge of pastel particles and blew past her as fast as he could.

She hated him. Usually, they got on okay. But today she hated him because he was right. Even if she did register a complaint about the untimely culling of her soul mate, the paperwork to start the process would fell a hundred trees and take a thousand years. The Celestial Plain had the bureaucracy from hell, except that Hell was super efficient.

Hades always got the cunning bastards. The ones who thought they could sneak and steal their way through life. And they did. It's the afterlife they forgot about. Wave a few dollars under their noses and they'd sneeze out their everlasting souls like so much sputum. So while Hell filled up with the sly and corrupt, the heavens had a glut of charity workers, animal activists, and for some reason, natural therapists. The last time Soul Selector looked in at the Office of Appeal, the top ticket on the inbox was a reprieve for Joan of Arc.

Death pulled a fast one running off like that. He knew how hopeless the situation was. Soul Selector would have to pull a few strings. Maybe she could ask for a private audience with Aphrodite, the Goddess of Love and her boss. After all, this was an emergency. Nevertheless, she balked at that option. The less the Gods knew the better for those who worked for them. Time was on her side. If she was lucky, maybe she could fix this herself, with or without Death's help. She had one half of a soul match languishing below and who knew where the dead half would show up? Soul Selector had to locate her, and quickly. She could still be operational.

CHAPTER SEVENTEEN

Jesse found herself sitting in a huge meadow surrounded by buttercups and sweet grass. *I don't know what just happened, but I think I fucked up.*

She had a headache and felt dull and unfocused. There'd been an accident. She knew that much. She carefully flexed her neck from side to side. Then her back. Next, she stretched out her arms and then her legs. She felt okay. She felt very okay, loose and limber, as if she'd finished a long swim session.

So I'm still in one piece. Without thinking, she broke a stem of grass to chew on and looked around her. *Well, it's not like it's awful or anything so I'm probably not in hell. But then again, it's not very heavenly either. Maybe I'm in the hospital and this is where the comatose hang out? Any minute now I'll hear my favorite song played on a loop.*

Wherever she was, it had the heavy, hazy feel of a lazy summer afternoon. It wasn't weird or unpleasant; it was just big. Very, very big. The meadow stretched away in every direction to impossibly distant indigo-smudged horizons. She was sitting in a huge prairie of rippling grass. Jesse was mesmerized by the wind-woven patterns falling open and closed in the grasses around her. She was transfixed by the flash of silver and greens swimming across the prairie like seawater when she realized there was no wind. The air lay heavy and still on her skin and the grass moved by itself like a living thing.

I'm dead. The thought exploded in her head. The sudden knowledge was irrefutable. *I'm dead. I died. And maybe that's okay.* She felt calm, apart from a small hand tremor. It was curious how deep the calm went within her. Like a drug seeping into her bones leaving her mellow but super receptive to her environment.

The dog wasn't with her. She spun a slow three hundred and sixty degrees but didn't see him. *At least one of us made it. Unless dogs go somewhere else? Which would be a pity because a dog would love it here.*

"Hello." The deep voice came from behind her.

Jesse turned to face the tallest woman with the bluest eyes she had ever seen. So blue it looked like the sky behind her had found a way to shine directly through her skull and blaze through her irises.

"Are you a giant?" Jesse asked in a voice squeaky with surprise.

The woman frowned. "No, I am the Soul Selector. The giants are over there in the Titan marshes." She pointed vaguely to the left.

"I meant that you're very tall."

The Soul Selector sniffed. "I'm just over nine foot, and you are sitting down."

"Did you select me? Is that why I'm here? You said you were a soul selecta—"

"No, I damn well did not select you. You are here because you have broken your eternal pathway and nobody knows what to do with you. And it's Soul Selector, with a TOR, not a TAH. Selec*tor*."

Jesse shrugged. "Whatever."

There was a moment's silence then Soul Selector asked, "What is a soul selecta?"

"A soul selecta is a deejay," Jesse said. "She selects the smoothest grooves. Keeps it chill. Manages the mood. Basically, a good one owns the place."

"Hmm." The sound was almost a growl. Soul Selector's scowl deepened as she thought this over. Then she seemed to resolve something and her frown quickly cleared. "Well, I am the Soul Selector. There are rules, you know."

"Okay, sure." Jesse was relieved the moment had passed. She was still trying to figure out if this scary chick was dangerous. What with the billowing black cloak and long dark hair, she looked like a banshee, and those luminescent blue eyes were freaky.

"So, how did I break my eternal pathway?" she said. "Is that why I'm here? And where exactly is here?"

"You are in the Elysian Fields on a sort of stopover," Soul Selector said. Her displeasure shone through. "It seems you've managed to jump the gun, fore sold on your allotted time, beat the clock, nipped out for an early lunch…you get the idea. And therefore, there is, as yet, no set place for you in Infinity. You'll just have to hang around here until the paperwork catches up with you." She sounded particularly peeved about the paperwork, which Jesse found a little unfair considering she'd just been told she was prematurely dead.

"I never expected the afterlife to be so bureaucratic."

"Oh, it is." Soul Selector snorted derisively. "I have just spent the last four years filling out your appeal form."

"Four years? But I've only just got here!"

"I'm afraid not. It doesn't work that way. Time is softer here."

"Softer?"

"Yes, like…like water pH types. They range between hard and soft. It's the same with time. It's softer here so it's much more fluid. It can flow unrestricted. In your…past reality…you had hard time. It's very viscous, full of toxins, and not very nice to live in. Does bad things to the body." She shrugged as if it should all be obvious.

"So I'm really dead?" Jesse still needed clarification.

"Yes, indeed you are. You made damn sure of that."

"And four years have passed since I died?"

"Four years of paperwork."

"Well, fuck that. Especially since I'm not supposed to be dead at all."

"Look, I tried to reverse it, but the paperwork..." Soul Selector shifted uncomfortably. "Trust me," she began again. "It's better this way. Look on the bright side. You're already buried." Her face took on a sort of cramped look that Jesse interpreted as a smile. Jesse did not smile back. Soul Selector shifted again.

"It's not that bad," she said. "Now you don't have to hang around at your funeral feeling guilty for all the upset you've caused your nearest and dearest. Most corpses hate that part. You'd be surprised how many of the dearly departed choose to do that and feel awful afterward." This was met by silence, so she unwisely continued, "I mean, it's been four years and everyone's got over it by now and moved on. You're practically forgotten." The cramp tightened across Soul Selector's face, and Jesse interpreted this as the smile brightening. "So, as a dead person, you need to move on, too. At least you will if I can find somewhere to stick you." This last part was a mutter. Her face lost its rictus and returned to its usual woebegone, somber state.

"Oh." Jesse was swamped with a deep, aching sadness. She felt emptied out. She was dead. Life was over. Her eyes welled up and she concentrated hard on the grass stem clutched between her fingers.

Soul Selector looked down at the young woman, no more than a girl really, and sighed. She flopped down on the embankment beside her. She wasn't very good at the touchy-feely stuff. There were trained meeters and greeters for the recently deceased. It was their job to soothe away the fears and regrets, not hers. As the Soul Selector, she had another skill set entirely. She glanced sideways at Jesse; the kid was in a bit of a state. She hoped there'd be no hugging.

"Well, can I at least see Mom and Dad? After all, it's been four years since…since the funeral." Jesse rubbed her eyes on her sleeve.

"No. You can't see anyone you used to know. It's the rules. It will only hold you back from moving on with your… new life…" Soul Selector tailed off awkwardly. Actually, she was unsure of the rules for this situation but had an idea that everything Jesse asked for should generally be denied.

"Oh." Jesse digested this. "I suppose it makes sense, but I really, really need to go back." There was passion in her voice, a strength of conviction that made Soul Selector shift in her shoes. "It's a sort of compulsion," Jesse continued. "I just know I have to go back. It's weird, but I feel like I'm not done, like I'm only part-baked, or something?"

Soul Selector started plucking at the grass as well. The kid was right; she was only part-lived. There'd been another destiny for her entirely, and now that was broken and Soul Selector didn't know what to do about it, apart from fill in complaint forms. Death should sort this mess out. It was not her job.

"Hey, maybe I could be a ghost?" Jesse asked.

"No." Soul Selector damped down that idea at once. "Ghosts are vengeful spirits with earthly agendas. They like lingering and are always griping on about being murdered." Soul Selector began to chew on her stalk of grass. "You're never going to be a ghost. What you did was just plain stupid. We might have caught a break if you'd been murdered."

"All I did was rescue a dog. It was the right thing to do."

"Not if you ended up here, it wasn't. We have a special room for hero types, and you're not in it."

"Is that why I'm here? I'm a failed hero. Is this a sort of purgatory for losers?"

"No, it is not. This is the Elysian Fields, and you are here because…" Soul Selector ran out of words. *Because you shouldn't be dead, you should be down on earth with the love of your life pumping good energy out into the universe. Gods feed on good energy; you don't want to be around them when it starts to run out. But I'm not allowed to tell you that.* "Because there's rules and you broke them."

"Look," Jesse said. "I need to know what's going on back home. Please?"

"The need will pass. You're in a period of adjustment, that's all. I bet if I come by here in another fifteen years you'll be a lot more relaxed."

"Fifteen years!"

"I told you before, this is soft time. Fifteen years is a doddle."

"What am I going do here for fifteen years?"

Soul Selector shrugged and looked around the vast, verdant expanse. "Frisbee?"

"By myself?"

"Maybe we can find that dog you failed to save." Her tone hardened.

"Fuck you." Jesse stormed to her feet and marched off.

"Brilliant. A brat," Soul Selector muttered. "What am I supposed to do with a brat? I'm not a meet-n-greeter. It's not my job to babysit the overly sensitive deceased." She flung down her grass stalk and stomped off after her charge.

CHAPTER EIGHTEEN

After a few minutes of full, head down charging, Jesse stopped and looked around. She must be at least two miles away from the slope she'd sat on only moments ago.

"What's with this fucked up place?" she shouted at the far horizons.

"This fucked up place is a department of the afterlife. The Elysian Fields to be exact." The response came from directly beside her. The Soul Selector stood by her shoulder.

"How did I get here?"

"You died without permission. Went AWOL on life, gave up the ghost, went knocking on heaven's door—"

"Not here. Here?" Jesse pointed to the ground under her feet. "A moment ago, I was over there." She pointed toward the embankment. "It's miles away."

"Oh, it's another space-time thingy. We got it all going on up here. Soft time, hard time, squishy dimensions. Jesse, step away from the pool!" Soul Selector's eyes widened with anxiety. Her gaze was fixed on the spot where Jesse stood.

Jesse took a nervous half step backward and found herself wobbling on the edge of a small muddy pool. She regained her balance and peered at the reed-rimmed waterhole. It didn't look that dangerous.

"Is this where the animals come to drink?" She gestured at the brackish water. Maybe the animals were dangerous?

"Animals?" Soul Selector looked horrified. "At my pool? I should think not."

Jesse frowned. The pool was weird. The water seemed to absorb light. Nothing was reflected back, not even the bright, cloudless sky.

"Come away," Soul Selector said. The slight plea in her voice made Jesse hesitate. Something was going on here, something special. She could feel it. And the weird chick didn't want her to know what it was. That made her stick her heels in even more.

"How deep is it?" She toed at the water with her sneaker, and a myriad of startled ripples ran away from her. Out in the center, where it was deeper, the water rolled unhappily, as if it was alive and not happy that she'd kicked it. Jesse shivered. It was creepy. "Can you swim in it?" Not that she'd want to.

Soul Selector actually spluttered. "Swim? You certainly cannot! This is a scrying pool. Stay out of it. And stop touching it."

"A what pool?" Jesse toed the water again, only gently. The pool shivered back at her. A thrill ran through her and the water rippled, mirroring her tremor.

"A scrying pool. It's for divining…well, sort of. Stop poking it. You're waking it up."

"Divining? Like fortune telling?" Jesse was fascinated. Something sentient definitely lived in the water. She could feel it stir. "What do you mean I'm waking it up? It's only water." She wanted Soul Selector to confirm what she already guessed, that the pool was alive and watchful.

"It's more than water. It's like a window. It lets me keep an eye on my charges. Or in this case, charge, singular." Soul Selector's initial fluster flipped over to bossiness. "Get away from it. It's not for you."

"A window to another dimension? Cool. How does it work?" Jesse squinted into the depths. The water swirled then, somewhere beneath its surface, it parted like theater curtains revealing a stage set of a small cafe in New York. "Hey, look, I can see someone."

"What!"

"A girl. I can see a girl with blond hair."

"No! No, no, no. You can't."

"She's very pretty." Jesse was mesmerized by the opaque forms floating before her.

"You can't see her. It's a trick of the light."

"Nope, no trick. There's definitely a girl in there. Well, a young woman." Jesse let her knees sink into the mud. Her gaze was locked on the ephemeral vision of the young woman. She was sipping chai tea and engrossed in a biography of Edith Piaf.

"Wait a minute," Soul Selector said. "You mean to tell me you can actually see something, someone…in there?" *Please. Not this on top of everything else. This child is utterly impossible to work with.*

There was no way a simple soul like Jesse should be able to scry in her pool without at least a millennia of lessons. It had taken Soul Selector over three thousand years to get her diploma, and even now she was barely able to keep track of her charges. Hence the "Day of the Dog" incident. She had taken her eye off Jesse Colvin for one hard time minute, and look what happened. How often had she stared into this watery murk until her eyeballs cramped trying to make out if it were night or day?

And now this little space-time orphan comes along, plops herself down, and can suddenly SEE things. No way. It has to be some sort of joke. Soul Selector surreptitiously looked around for Hermes. He fancied himself as a bit of a trickster when he was nothing but annoying. There was no one else at the pool, just herself and Jesse who was flat on her muddy belly watching the living reflection of her lost mate. Thank Zeus the girl had no idea who she was actually looking at.

"I see a young woman. She's blond and petite. And very lonely. She's feeling lost." Jesse pulled back in confusion, "I can see her. I mean really see her, like inside of her. What she's feeling, what her thoughts are." She looked over at Soul Selector for confirmation. "It's as if I can touch her soul," she said in wonder.

Soul Selector groaned. *It's that damned vibe connection experiment. It's got to be that. I need to bin it before it haunts me for all eternity.*

"She's a beautiful person, inside and out. I can sense it. I can see her beauty through more than my eyes. It's like my soul knows these things." Jesse was awestruck. "Is this what the pool is for? Is that how you use it?"

"Sort of. But you shouldn't be looking! You need...um... security clearance. Yes. And you've not got any, so stop it." She gestured with her thumb. "Come on, up and out of it. You're not allowed and that's final." She made to grab Jesse's arm and haul her up. Jesse hung on like a dead weight, refusing to move, unwilling to let go of her vision.

"I'm doing no harm. I want to see what happens to her. It's important. I know it is." She sounded determined. "Who is she?"

"Somebody. Nobody. Just a person I'm keeping an eye on. None of your concern." Soul Selector managed to drag Jesse away. "Come on, you're breaking the rules. Get up and let me show you around."

"Your rules suck."

"My rules are perfectly good for what they're needed for. For instance keeping you away from my pool." The last thing she needed was for these two souls to start all that bonding business again, especially with Jesse on a celestial plane. There was no way these two could get around the fact Jesse was deceased, so there was no point in letting Jesse know the woman she was ogling was her lost soul mate.

Lost being the operative word. It was unfortunate, but Norrie Maguire was a doomed soul. The thread had been cut. She was now a destiny set adrift. A fate wasted.

It would be cruel for Jesse to learn the truth. And it would lead to all sorts of complicated questions Soul Selector had no wish to deal with. Best to let the Celestial collective make up its mind and sort the whole sorry mess out.

Soul Selector felt satisfied she was doing the best she could in the circumstances. She had acted with sensitivity toward her unwanted guest. She had welcomed her to her under-prepared afterlife. She had been kind and honorable. Her next step was to drug the girl.

Let Jesse sleep away the next hundred thousand years or so, and maybe when she woke up she'd have forgotten the whole thing? Even better, maybe her little soul mate friend would have died and be due for reincarnation. With any luck, they would be in sync and all she would have to do is shove them both into the reincarnation queue before anyone noticed a big hunk of love energy was missing. The Gods loved their manna. One bite less and there would be all sorts of questions.

Yes, drug Jesse, that was the thing to do. For the first time, Soul Selector allowed herself a shred of hope. Finally, she had a plan that might bring the whole sorry affair under her control.

CHAPTER NINETEEN

Sʇ ee those trees?" Soul Selector pointed to a blue haze
about twenty miles or more to the east.

Jesse squinted in the bright afternoon glare. "Yeah, I see
them."

And then they were there standing in the dappled shade of a
small copse surrounded by fruit trees of every variety.

"Wow. Did we just teleport or something?"

"It's how we travel around here. Space is hard and soft,
too."

"Can I do that?"

"Maybe later." Soul Selector was getting impatient. "Now,
this is the Orchard of Obliv—Of…Obis."

"Obis? You were going to say oblivion, weren't you?"

"No, I wasn't. This is the Orchard of Obis, and isn't it
lovely? It has some nice fruit. Very tasty. You really have to try
some."

"What's an obis?"

"It's a sash belt on a kimono." Soul Selector's left eye
twitched several times in rapid succession. She was becoming
irritated. Jesse was hard work. This was the first time she had
come up close to a soul mate, and they were annoying little
things.

"What's a kimono got to do with fruit?"

Soul Selector ignored the question. "I want you to snack here as often as you feel like. Any time, night or day, feel free to help yourself from any tree." She spread her hands indulgently. "Any of them."

"I don't think I'll get used to this way of travel," Jesse murmured, rubbing her stomach. "It's making me queasy. I don't want to eat anything." She looked around in interest.

"You'll get used to it. Anyway, you'll not want to move far from the orchard. It's nice here, very restful. Why not take a nap in the shade?"

"I'm not sleepy. Can we go back to the pool?"

Soul Selector's left eye pulsed. "No," she said. "Have an orange." She reached out pale, bony fingers and plucked one from a tree. "It's so juicy and sweet." She threw it awkwardly toward Jesse who caught it deftly in one hand. "Go on, eat." Soul Selector made little encouraging movements with her hands.

"Orchard of Obis, eh?" Jesse tossed the orange casually from one hand to the other. Soul Selector watched it arc back and forth anxiously. "My mother told me about strangers and candy. And she never let up about spiked drinks."

"Huh?" Soul Selector was still focused on the orange.

Jesse wasn't stupid. She knew the fruit was drugged. This orchard was more like the copse of collapse. The poor bees were falling from the blossoms and crawling drunkenly across the ground. And Soulie here had the worst poker face imaginable. It was laughable how earnest she tried to look. The longer Jesse hung out with her, the less scary the neon-eyed chick became. In fact, the whole Grim Reaper ensemble looked stupid once she noticed the klutz inside it.

"Catch." She tossed the orange toward Soul Selector, pitching it perfectly, then spun on her heel and ran farther into the trees. "Back to me," she shouted over her shoulder. "First to drop it eats it."

Soul Selector caught the orange by pure reflex. Reflexes she didn't know she had. How odd. Nothing was as simple or straightforward as it used to be since Jesse arrived.

Soul Selector hesitated, uncertain what to do. Jesse darted through the trees shouting for the orange to be thrown back.

"Cheeky little so-and-so." Soul Selector drew back her arm and, much to her delight, made a decent pitch back.

It was easily dealt with by the younger woman, and before Soul Selector could blink, the orange came hurtling back at her with a spin on it that stung the palm of her hand.

"Is that the best you can do?" Jesse taunted her, and ran for the edge of the orchard. Soul Selector followed. They burst out of the grove onto the open plain and continued to throw the orange back and forth to each other.

Soul Selector enjoyed the gentle exercise. She was stretching muscles that had been bunched up too tight for more time than she knew. Her cloak billowed out behind her in the breeze, spinning and lifting until the cloth cracked around her ears. This was fun! *Fun?* Fun was another alien sensation that had popped up from nowhere. It added extra pace in her step, and her face relaxed out of its usual grimace. Even her eye stopped twitching. Maybe fun wasn't such a bad thing after all.

An undertone drifted in on the bustling wind. A low whine that soon became the buzz of an annoying insect. It was dull and monotonous but with enough insistence to drill through the playful slap of her cloak and the rustle of grass. It gradually built in volume until Soul Selector stopped to cock an ear to the wind.

"Time out," she called. "I'm getting a fax." A second later, she said, "I need to go. I'm late for a meeting." She tossed the orange back gently. "Look, Jesse, eat the orange. I'll be back soon. Promise."

"Like when?" The orange fell to the grass. Jesse didn't want to lose her one and only companion. The Elysian Fields were intimidating with their big skies and endless grasslands. The sheer magnitude of everything was overwhelming. Besides, she was having genuine fun and suspected Soul Selector was enjoying the game, too.

"Um, twenty years give or take. Good-bye."

"What? Wait!" Jesse called out in desperation, but Soul Selector had gone. The space she had occupied hazed like a mirage then refocused with a snap back to the crystalline daylight of the surrounding prairie. Jesse stood alone in a sea of weaving grass. Behind her, the orchard trees whispered alluringly, promising shelter and shade and heaven knew what else. The breeze caressed her face, drying the sweat on her brow. The same breeze that apparently was an office fax for Soul Selector but had no message for Jesse.

"Twenty fucking years?" she yelled at the horizon. "I'm gonna die of boredom in this fucking field!"

Except she already was dead. Panic rose. Her throat went tight. She looked around her. This was it. This was her eternity. She was in the middle of thousands and thousands of acres of… what? Afterlife, heaven, nothingness, and hallucinating about a crazy woman in a cloak. There was nothing for miles and miles and miles but prairie. She'd never survive. She'd already failed to survive.

How could there be no one else here? Where were all the other dead people? There were more dead than living so why was she alone? Soul Selector was keeping secrets from her, and Jesse needed answers and there was only one place she knew where she might find them.

She looked to the distant embankment where she had first arrived. The pool was close to that spot. The only time she'd felt safe and content was when she had gazed into it. She wanted to go back to the pool. But how?

The slope was maybe twenty miles away from the orchard sitting in its own little heat haze. What was it Soul Selector had said about moving about here? That she'd get used to it! Did that mean she should be able to do it? Jesse squeezed her eyes shut and concentrated hard on where she wanted to be. She opened one eye to peek. She was still at the orchard.

She tried again. Still nothing. She began to feel stupid. Fuck it, she would walk, and if it took a hundred years, so what? If it took a thousand years, so what? A hundred, thousand, million, billion years, so what? She was in a fucking unending prairie all alone so she might as well take a stroll.

Jesse slumped onto the grass, spread-eagled below the vast, empty skies. She was nothing in the enormity of it all. She blinked back tears and tried to be strong. Look on the bright side. Find the positives, like she'd always wanted to learn to meditate and this was the perfect place.

She sat up, leaning back on her hands and held her face to the sky and took slow, deep breaths. Her weight shifted and her hand slid out from under her into water. Jesse pulled back, startled, and stared at her wet palm. Water! She twisted around to look behind her. She was at the pool! Right beside it at the exact spot she had been earlier.

Jesse checked the horizon and saw the orchard. It was a smoky dot on the distant skyline. She'd done it. She'd teleported. That meant she could get around this gods-forsaken dump to anywhere she wanted. Though how she'd actually managed to do it was another matter. Her elation was further dampened by the realization there was nowhere else she wanted to be, except here, by this little pool.

Jesse leaned over the water's edge and focused, anxious that her previous vision had been a fluke. She so wanted to see the young woman again. She felt compelled to see her. What if she saw nothing but her own fear-filled face reflected back? She held her breath, eyes wide, straining for a vision to appear. The wind chopped up the surface of the water and the reeds hissed around her. There was nothing to see. It was all one big joke. This entire place was her own private hell. Tears rose to choke her and she fought them back.

Over the creak of bending reeds came the soft tinkling of wind chimes. It was a totally displaced sound. Jesse looked all around her. Where was it coming from? Was it her imagination and she was finally going mad? She wouldn't be surprised. Around her, there was nothing but prairie grass swaying outward and away from her in all directions, as if she were the iris in an eye of grass.

The wind chimes faded away, and her heart sank. The sound was lost before she had found its source. On the next gust of wind, the disjointed melody returned. Still she couldn't locate it. She looked to where the orchard lay and beyond that the blue-gray horizon. She glanced back at the pool. Bright sunlight and sea surf bubbled under the surface of what, until a moment ago, had been dark, muddy water. Jesse flung herself belly down and gazed in wonder at the beach vista cradled within the scrying pool. The wind chimes took on the deeper, more melodious tone of a piano. Music filled the air around the pool. It hovered and hung like the sea birds in the tableau before her. Then each musical note began to crystallize like the drops of seawater shimmering on the edge of the curling waves.

The scene shifted to a house on the shore. Jesse wasn't sure how she knew, but the woman she saw at the piano was the same one as earlier, only older. It was an innate knowledge that told her the woman was playing the piano in her own home, and that the location was the west coast of Ireland. It was a beautiful home overlooking a vast dune-filled beach. The hot prairie winds changed direction, and Jesse tasted salt on her tongue. The cool sea breeze kissed her brow. The woman sat by open terrace doors. A breeze played with the muslin curtains and lifted the sheet music on her piano. Jesse noticed the woman wasn't reading the music, she was writing it. Every so often she would pause and lift a small silver pencil and make marks on the manuscript. Jesse was captivated. Who was she?

Whoever she was, Jesse felt an uncanny attachment to her. It was as if an invisible thread pulled her so far forward she could fall in the pool and drown. And she would willingly do so if it meant she would be closer. It was torture to be so near and yet so far from her.

Who was she?

CHAPTER TWENTY

Norrie ran her fingers over the piano keys and filled her seafront home with music. A delicious tingle ran over her skin, and the fine hair on her forearms rose. The composition was more than good. She could feel it already. This song was special, and rightly so as it was for a special cause.

Apart from the piano, the only other sound was the distant surf and the call of seabirds, each blending perfectly with the ballad she was crafting. Norrie rested her hands on the keys as the last notes faded away and let her gaze wander to the foam-topped waves. A breeze stirred the curtains by the terrace doors and feathered her cheeks. It wasn't until it started shifting the sheet music on her piano top that she dropped out of her reverie and went to close the doors. She hesitated on the terrace steps to enjoy the view. The Irish light changed so quickly, re-creating the panorama before her in an instant.

A dog walker threw a stick into the tide and his dog plunged in after it. The dog owner was the only human being she had seen all day and exactly why she had chosen to build her home on the coast. Norrie loved the solitude she found here. It allowed countless complex emotions to slowly surface and weave their way into her music. Her gaze shifted to where sea met sky in a smudge of dark Atlantic gray, and she let her thoughts drift until words and rhythms teased together, and she had her lyrics. The new song would be about sand and sea and salt with the crack of marram grass as its backbone. It was exciting and it would totally work.

A charity had approached her to help with fundraising, and she had agreed to write a special song for them. Truth was, she was enjoying the challenge. Today she had completed the first draft and already had a strong idea of where she was going on the production side. So many people in the industry either owed her a favor or were angling to work with her that she knew it would be easy to pull in some big names to front it. Already she had that buzz that told her this was going to be something big, something she'd be proud of.

Her thoughts turned to Loa Ebele, her contact for the charity. She was just getting to know Loa and felt enormous respect for her work and her personal and professional integrity. Norrie looked forward to their next informal meeting. She'd been thinking of Loa a lot recently. It was funny the way she had slipped into Norrie's everyday thoughts, until the next thing she knew her perceptions had gently shifted until her being seemed to pause and shiver, only to softly rebalance. She imagined it like sand flowing down a dune, grain by grain, slowly at first, moving like silk, but once started it was unstoppable. Her fingers played with a knot in the oak wood of the terrace railing. *I wonder if love is like that?*

Immediately, she felt embarrassed. She was meeting Loa for coffee later that afternoon and admitted she was looking forward to it, perhaps more than she ought to. She had to be careful. She could feel the flutter of mutual attraction between them, and it worried her. She knew from past experience falling in love was not a cure; it was distraction. One she enjoyed but could not necessarily afford.

❖

"I should be back on the twentieth," Norrie murmured into her coffee cup. She shared a shy smile with Loa sitting across from her. Loa smiled back. Her eyes were warm as melting caramel and held the essence of her smile as much as the curve of her lips did.

"New York and Nashville. Man, it sounds glamorous," she said.

"It isn't. It's tiring but necessary. And I'd like to run the charity song past you sometime soon. Though remember it's still embryonic."

"I'm so excited about it," Loa said. "Would you like to visit the clinic with me when you get back? Meet some of the people you're helping?"

"I'd love to. I really would." She sounded too eager and hoped Loa thought it was for the right reasons. Loa was lovely. Her conversation was intelligent and entertaining and she was fun to be around, and that made Norrie anxious. She was attracted to Loa. She wanted to be. She had felt this way about many women. She'd had many love affairs. Her anxiety came from a profound fear of disappointment. Norrie drifted into relationships in a happy bubble of make-believe. She wanted to be in love. And she wanted it to be a real and forever thing. But each time, something didn't feel quite right. Love was like a new shoe that never grew out of its pinch.

Her expectations were undefined and unfocused. She was looking for a special feeling that she couldn't transcribe, and that's what scared her. The flip side of special was a terrible, unfathomable need and the depression that dogged it.

Across the table, Loa smiled. Her whole face lit up, and her eyes, fringed with the thickest lashes Norrie had ever seen, sparkled like a child's. Loa's smile was the antithesis of the agitation eating Norrie. She wanted to drown in Loa's eyes as much as she wanted to be rescued by her. It wasn't fair to place Loa in this position. She was a kind, beautiful person. She didn't deserve a mess like Norrie in her life. She hesitated, tasting anxiety in the dryness of her mouth, then she took a deep breath and smiled right back.

Chapter Twenty-one

"What in Hades kept you? I've been waiting for ages. When I summon someone, they better get here quick!" Aphrodite's voice reverberated off the marble columns of her divine temple and rattled the ears of the handmaidens draped gracefully around her feet. They flinched, teeth grinding behind their winsome smiles.

Aphrodite's temple floated in the heavens. The temple columns stretched so high they disappeared in cloudbanks. The walls opened wide onto the brilliant blue of a perpetual summer sky. Nymphs adorned it. Doves flew through it. The winds wailed. It was a thing of beauty. It gave Soul Selector vertigo.

Her stomach was sour, too. Almost as sour as the beautiful face on the throne before her. Most people had a different take as to what the Goddess of Love was like. Soul Selector knew they were wrong. Aphrodite was a hard-assed bitch to work for. A constant reminder that the most vivid snakes were also the most venomous. But then, as the Goddess herself would say, love hurts.

At this moment her divine loveliness's face was suffused with an ugly red color, yet she still managed to look hot, bothered, and gorgeous. Eros stood at her side picking his acne. Soul Selector didn't like him. He was a punk, so she ignored him and bowed to his mother alone. Aphrodite was head of her department and the only one she answered to.

"It's a soft time thing." She tried to pacify the Goddess. It was surprising how many Gods didn't get the soft time, hard time thing even though they lived with it every day. "I've only just received your request and—"

"Summons. I summoned you. I *never* request. And shut up. The only soft thing around here is your head."

Eros sniggered, and Soul Selector shot him a look. He clammed up, but not before attempting to glare back. It came across as weak and sullen, and he only dared to try because his mother was close by. Normally, he was nervous around her flint-eyed stares.

Aphrodite's cheeks turned even blotchier and her sea-foam green eyes stormed. In the world below, oceans roiled and sailors prayed, but she didn't care. She was as cruel as she was beautiful. Men could drown in her eyes as easily as the seas that birthed her. She was unmoved. Soul Selector focused hard on the swirls in the marble floor. It was too easy to become mesmerized by her, and that was when the trouble started. The floor rocked under her feet and the whole temple swayed in the increasing winds. She stumbled for balance and noticed the nymphs staggered, too. Water sloshed from the feature fountain in the center of the temple, agitating the swans that swam in it, until they flapped their huge wings and honked with alarm. Aphrodite was in a terrible mood, and everyone knew it.

"What's this I hear about a deficit?" she yelled. "Can't you do anything right? There's a shortfall, and I'm getting it in the neck from this lot!" She jerked her thumb angrily to the right. "These friggers never give me a moment's peace. It's constant whine, whine, whine."

Soul Selector followed the direction of her thumb but could only see Ares fast asleep on a well padded couch and assumed he was the token representative of all the other friggers currently beleaguering Aphrodite. A few bored Nereids fanned him with palm fronds, though they looked like they'd rather be beating him with them. He wouldn't have felt a thing. Ares was a large man, as well padded as the couch he was unattractively splayed on. A fat, lazy god, he was far too idle to properly oversee the destruction he wreaked. That's why most wars dragged on forever. Ares was too useless to bring even the smallest skirmish to proper closure.

"This couldn't have come at a worse time. You know the events calendar is rammed," Aphrodite said. The festival of Dionysius was fast approaching, and the gods needed their manna. To them manna was pudding, cookies, and beer all rolled into one, and only soul love provided it. Lots and lots of soul love. It was their gear oil. It gave them the energy to operate and to keep the world turning. "And now I hear we have an unscheduled visitor in the Fields. Get rid."

"Get rid?" Soul Selector hated the wobble in her voice, but Aphrodite unnerved her. She often found the Goddess's conversation hard to follow.

"Yes. Put it in the recycling bin or whatever. Just lose it," Aphrodite said.

"But...but, she's a soul mate. I'm trying to correct the situation. I've filled out the required forms, and I'm waiting—"

"Why are we still talking? Why do I have to repeat everything I say? Once again, you have fucked up and left me in an embarrassing position." Aphrodite stopped abruptly. She looked annoyed, as if she'd said too much.

Soul Selector wasn't sure what Aphrodite was referring to. To her knowledge, she'd never "fucked up," and in this instance, if anyone had, it was Death not her. He had fucked up rather royally where Jesse was concerned.

"Dump it." Aphrodite's eyes narrowed to icy slits. In the world below, an Arctic ice sheet shattered.

"Dump the soul? But she's not due for recycl—reincarnation for at least several hundred years." Soul Selector was flustered. She didn't understand. "There are rules."

"Repeeeeetinngggg." Aphrodite used a singsong voice that was more menacing than musical. This couldn't be right. Dump a soul mate? Soul Selector's lips quivered, but luckily no words formed.

Ares gave a snort, rolled over on his couch, and farted. The Nereids recoiled, and Soul Selector used the distraction to melt away.

CHAPTER TWENTY-TWO

Norrie hated hospitals. As a young girl, the harsh antiseptic odors had added to her panic on every visit. Now, in the brand new wing of Our Lady of Lourdes, the smell of fresh paint and vinyl floor tiles clawed at her gut even though it was a bright and cheerful place. Despite the memories, Norrie had to suppress a giggle at her squeaky shoe soles on the new floor. The signs for the hepatology ward seemed to run on forever, but eventually, she squeaked around the last corner to find Loa waiting for her by the nurses' station.

"Hey." She smiled as they hugged. "Did you hear me coming?"

"I can hear Michael Kors moccasins from a mile away."

"That's weird. Yet curiously classy." The hug was a microsecond too long. She saw that Loa noticed too and drew away awkwardly.

"I also know a Valentino shirt when I hug one."

"Stop reading my labels." Norrie laughed and touched the back of her collar self-consciously.

"I'm not. There's a V on your breast pocket." Loa pointed it out. She gave a cheeky grin and said, "Come and meet my kids."

The floor of the children's ward was littered with toys. Runaway balloons hung from the ceiling tiles. There were four beds in the small room with three children sitting on the floor playing a board game. The children's ages varied. Norrie guessed the youngest was around seven or eight but small for her age. The other two were a boy and girl both in their early teens. They played patiently with the younger girl who was fidgety and non-attentive. All three looked up as Loa and Norrie entered.

"Loa!" The youngest girl struggled to her feet. She moved clumsily, and Norrie could see it took her some effort.

"Good morning, Oona." Loa drew the girl into a big hug. The teenagers also rose to greet her. "Hi, guys. What are you playing?"

"Risk, but it's boring," Oona answered on behalf of everybody. She still clung to Loa.

"Norrie, meet Ross and Michaela, and this little monkey is Oona," Loa said. She didn't seem to mind Oona draped around her waist.

Norrie wished them all good morning, noted a violent flush cover Michaela's cheeks, and knew she'd been recognized by her.

"Loa told us you were helping with the fundraiser," Michaela said. "I love your music. I have all your CDs."

"They must be pretty battered. I haven't recorded anything new for nearly six years," Norrie joked. The main audience for her heartbreak ballads had been ladies of a certain age, and Michaela failed that demographic by at least several years.

"My mam listens to you all the time. Would it be okay if I asked for an autograph? For my mam?"

"Of course." Norrie's smile widened. It made sense that Michaela had heard of her through her mother.

"Better yet, why not a photo for your mam?" Loa waggled her iPhone. "There'll be a proper PR campaign nearer the release date, but we could take a few pics now, just for fun." She looked at Norrie for an okay, but Norrie was already moving into a group hug, pulling everyone in closer and smiling brightly for the camera.

She had noticed the waxy pallor of the children's faces when she came into the ward, but up close, she could see it was jaundice pallor. Ross's and Michaela's eyes had a bruised, tired look with little strings of red where the capillaries had burst. And when Oona stood up straight, her swollen abdomen was obvious. She hung off Norrie as she had off Loa, but not with the gauche preteen neediness Norrie had at first presumed. The little girl clung to her in borderline exhaustion. Oona was fighting her tiredness. The distraction of their visitor had kept her on her feet longer than was wise or necessary, and now she was sagging at the knees.

The camera flashed, and immediately after, Loa ushered Oona to her bed. "Your parents are dropping in later," she said. "If you take a nap now you won't fall asleep while they're here. Deal?"

Oona didn't argue. She was happy to kick off her slippers and climb into bed. Ross started to clear away the board game, and Michaela hovered nearby, clearly starstruck.

"I'll send the photo to your phone so you can show your mother," Loa assured her. "Do you want a copy, Ross?"

He nodded eagerly and Loa started pressing buttons. Norrie found it interesting Loa kept these kids' phone numbers in her own phone. It underscored the friendliness she had witnessed between them. Loa really did go that extra mile for the people she was helping.

"I think I have some ancient promo packs at home from my last tour. I'll hunt them out and Loa can bring them over. If you want, that is?"

They did want, and on that promise, Loa escorted Norrie from the ward.

"They are wonderful kids," Norrie said. They were heading toward the main hall. "I'm honored to be helping them."

Loa stopped by the elevator doors. "Have you time for one more visit?" she asked. "There's someone I want you to meet. The one you might help the most."

"Of course." Norrie was intrigued. Especially when they entered the elevator and Loa pressed the button for the top floor.

"That was our new hepatology department. We share the rest of the ground floor with orthopedics and gynae. On the top floor are the labs and the ICU. I want to drop in there before our visit is over," Loa said. The elevator doors slid open on a similar corridor with a similar smell of newness. They approached the ICU nurses' station.

"I always bring a cake or biscuits or something," Loa said, producing a small box of cupcakes from her bag. "Though they get more than enough." She indicated a box of chocolates opened on the counter.

"Sure, we need all the calories we can get. It's frantic here." The charge nurse, a small, roly-poly woman, offered up the chocolate box.

"Norrie, let me introduce charge nurse Rose Connelly," Loa said, picking a chocolate from the box. "She runs this place like Dublin Central Station. Nothing comes in or goes out unless it's on her timetable."

"And I already know who you are," Rose told Norrie. "We all think it's wonderful what you're doing with the fundraising."

Norrie blushed. "It's my pleasure." And was offered a second chocolate.

"Is it okay to drop in on JC for a minute?" Loa asked. Rose agreed and they moved along to the ICU ward, which was quiet and pristine. From this one main ward, several smaller rooms opened off it.

"This is a local case." Loa indicated they enter a private side ward. "I'm hoping patients like JC will benefit from our high profile fundraising efforts, like your song."

The room was cool and colored by the drabness of the day outside. Rain ran in rivulets along the windowpanes, and overcast skies brought a dour stillness to the room. A woman lay in the solitary bed. She was motionless. Central and arterial lines led out from her covers. She was attached to a nasogastric tube as well as a ventilator.

"This is JC Waites," Loa said. "She's had an encephalopathic episode and is in a coma. JC was born with a damaged liver, and it's deteriorated over time."

"What will happen to her? How long has she been like this?"

"She's been in the coma only a few days. She had respiratory failure." Loa gazed compassionately at JC. "She's a truly lovely person, Norrie. If you met her I guarantee you'd like her. She's a civil engineer. In fact, she helped build the bridge you drove over to get here."

"What will they do if her liver is failing? A transplant?"

"She's on the transplant list already. That's where you come in," Loa said. "Your song will raise awareness of our waiting list. We need more donors. It's as simple as that."

"You know her then?" Norrie asked.

"Yes. I've known JC for years. She's been attending the clinic since her condition slowly began to destabilize, and before that she helped out with fundraising any way she could."

"Will she get a liver donation in time?"

"I hope so. It's touch and go." Loa stood by the bedside smoothing the coverlet. Norrie could see the strain on her face. It must be an impossible position, running the regional branch for a charity so connected to the well-being of a friend.

"We better go." Loa led Norrie from the room. "Before Rose throws us out."

Rose met them in the corridor. "I'm glad you came along to see her," she said to Norrie. "It's cruel that we can't do any more for her just yet." Then she asked, "How's the song coming along?"

"The first draft is done," Loa told her. "I'm going to hear it soon."

"When?" Rose asked.

"Why don't you come over this evening? I can play it for you then." Norrie spoke out before she thought and immediately panicked. Did she want this? Wasn't it too over familiar? Loa's face brightened, making Norrie feel the exact reverse. She was now uncommonly pleased she had offered. Rose clucked in approval.

"Maybe you can bring over a copy we can play to JC?" she said. "Lord knows what she picks up from the everyday world. It can hardly hurt." Norrie agreed she'd drop off a promo CD when she was happy with the quality. No promises as to when, though. These things took time. Rose seemed happy enough and left them to return to her duties.

"In fact, why don't you come for dinner?" Norrie felt a little braver.

"I'd love to. I really want to hear you play," Loa said, then confessed, "I watched a few clips on YouTube."

"Ugh." Norrie grimaced. "I sound better without a perm. Is eight thirty okay? I'm not a great cook, but I promise you a decent supper." She forced herself to relax. The evening would be what it would be. Loa was a lovely companion, and she was interested in getting her opinion on the song before she tinkered with it any more.

"Can I ask what it's about? What angle you took?" Loa said.

"It's about waiting for the tide to turn and for the day to dawn. Of course it's all allegorical. The dawn represents new life, and the tide, well, that's the wait, I suppose. I think it will work okay. It feels right to my ears, but I'd like you to hear it, too."

"I can't wait. Will I bring red or white?"

Norrie looked at her blankly for a moment. "Oh, wine." The penny dropped and she laughed. She could feel the tension between them. It was a cord of rawhide drying in the heat they were building, and it was slowly pulling them together. Her stomach hitched, and she concentrated on sensible, everyday thoughts. *I'll stop at the supermarket on the way home. What will I get for supper? Pasta? Pizza?* It didn't work. Already she could feel the soapy walls forming around her. Soon she would be floating in her little bubble above the rooftops, ignorant and uncaring of the fall beneath her. She needed to take this slow and not rush in and trample it to death. *Be sensible. Think sensible.*

"Bring red," she said.

Chapter Twenty-three

I spy with my little eye, something beginning with H. C."
Jesse rocked back on her heels startled by the voice behind her. A young man in a pastel green shell suit was leaning over her shoulder staring into the pool. His hands were on his knees for balance and his soft brown cheek was inches from her nose. He smelled of cinnamon and warm honey. The smell reminded her of the Sunday morning oatmeal her mother used to make.

"Who are you?"

"Oops, I didn't mean to startle you. I'm Death. How do you do?"

"Haven't we already met, seeing as how I'm dead and all."

"Ah. You've heard about that." He paused and looked all about him. "I like what you've done here."

Jesse looked around her. She was by the pool, but it was now in the shade of a cluster of jacaranda trees. The fine feathery leaves whispered in the breeze, and drooping panicles of purple flowers swung over her head. Large flat rocks circled the water, the dappled sunlight crazing them with warm, hazy, tortoise shell patterns.

"It wasn't like this a moment ago." She was awed by the change. Gone were the mud and the straggly sharp-edged reeds. This place was weird. Nothing was fixed down.

Death shrugged. "You must have made it like this. Sort of decorated it with your mind. I like the big wocks. They're much nicer for sitting on than the mud. You have some good ideas," he said with approval.

It was hard for her to register that this young man was death. He seemed so unthreatening. Gentleness and goodwill flowed through him like sunlight through linen on a washing line.

"Hepatic coma, by the way," he said.

Jesse stared at him blankly.

"That's what the H C was," he explained, pinking up a little. "I spy hepatic coma."

Jesse looked back to the hospital scenario. It was already fading. The white walls fell away until only a soft glow shone beneath the water.

"It's gone now," Death said, nodding at the pool. "You have to be quick." He sat down on a flat rock and made himself comfortable. "I like coming here to see what's going on. But don't tell Soulie. She'd have a fit."

"Hey. I call her that, too."

"She hates it."

"Good."

Death tittered behind his hand, and Jesse slowly warmed to him. He was as crazy as everything else around here.

"She does seem very territorial about her pool," she said, eyeing his pastel attire. "Is this your day off?"

"I'm not what you expected, am I?" His face sagged a little.

"Not really," she said.

"Most people are disappointed. They want a bit of pathos in their last moments, but I just can't do the Weeper thing."

"Weeper? Oh, Reaper. I see."

"Pathos doesn't work with a lisp." He shrugged nonchalantly but still managed to look embarrassed.

"I suppose I didn't expect you to look so...easygoing." Jesse chose her words carefully.

"Black is so not my color. Not with this skin tone," he confided. "And I hate that ugly old cloak, unlike someone we know." He giggled again.

"She does the Reaper thing much better what with that sour puss face. Pity you couldn't swap jobs."

"Oh my, no. It's not my thing. I like to have a little chat with my clients before we head off on the big one. It's much nicer that way."

"I don't remember having a chat with you."

"Ah." Death looked at her with apologetic, big brown eyes. "You weren't actually on my list. The dog was, but somehow you got in the way. Pity weally, especially as Soulie had a job for you. She's off trying to fix things wight now."

"I died instead of that stupid dog?" Jesse was outraged. "How can that happen?"

"Beats me. I've been over the paperwork a million times, and I've no idea how you did it. You must have found a loophole in the wools."

"The wools?"

"This is the afterlife. Of course there's wools. The higher powers make up the wools and we obey. Simple."

"Oh, rules." Jesse was getting the hang of his lisp. "What higher powers? You mean God?"

"Which one? There's thousands of them, old and new. These are the Elysian Fields on the Celestial Plains. The old gods wool here. Zeus, Hera, Poseidon, that lot. One big, crazy, dysfunctional family."

"You don't look that ancient."

"I moisturize." He stroked his shell-suited thigh. "And unlike others I could mention, I pay attention to what's going on below. Especially the latest fashions."

Jesse was unsure what fashion venues Death had been paying attention to; the bingo halls of Florida?

"Soul Selector told me I'd been dead for years. She yammered on about hard time and soft time and stuff like that and basically said I couldn't go back."

"She can be so negative sometimes." Death tutted. "She's so uptight, always has been."

"I'm dead here. Dead when I shouldn't be. I think I've got more to be uptight about. Can't you do something about it?"

Death shook his head. "You may be dead, but you're not in my department. You're a soul mate, so Soulie is the boss of you."

"I'm a soul mate?"

"Of course you are. Look at you, glued to this muck puddle. That woman you see, she's your other half."

"The one in the hepatic coma?" Jesse felt sick to her stomach. She was dead and her soul mate was in a coma. What shitty sort of happy ever after was this?

"No, silly. The blond one is your other half. I've no idea who's in the coma. She's not on my list so that's good news for her, eh?"

"I wasn't on your list either."

He sighed. "You're never going to let that go, are you?"

"Not for the foreseeable." Jesse turned back to the pool. She was excited. She had a soul mate. She longed to lie beside it in peace and while away eternity gazing at her. Her intense attachment to the woman made sense now. It also made her intense longing bittersweet. "Do you know what her name is?"

Death shrugged. "No idea. Not my department. Ask Soulie."

"So what's she doing about it? You said she was trying to fix things." There was so much hope in her voice it made her cringe to hear it. She had no faith in Soul Selector. The big weird chick didn't come across as a fixer type. She couldn't even trick the dead into eating drugged oranges. And as for Death, his aim was as awry as his fashion sense.

"I wouldn't hold my breath...oh, sorry." He giggled shyly. "I don't mean to joke. It just comes out that way. It's a nervous habit kind of thing." Death was surprisingly gentle, and not at all what she expected. She rather liked his awkwardness and super sensitivity.

"She was so mad at me," he continued. "I felt so bad, but there was nothing I could do. Honestly."

"It's okay. I'm too tired to care. I think Soul Selector got the worst of my mood," she said.

"It's not her day then. She's been summoned by Aphwodite, the queen of bitches."

"I thought Aphrodite was the goddess of love?"

"Oh, she is. But things are never as they seem here."

"Despite the wools?" Jesse stared glumly at the pool. It was still and impenetrable and it wasn't giving up any of its secrets while she had company.

Death nodded. "Despite the wools."

CHAPTER TWENTY-FOUR

A re you kidding me?"
"No!" Death said hotly, then, "What do you mean?"
"What are you doing here with her?" Soul Selector jerked
a finger to where Jesse hung over the pool. "You know I have
to wean her off it, yet here you are encouraging her to snoop."

"She was here when I arrived and had no twouble looking
in your pool. I think she's very clever. It took you ages to get the
hang of it."

"It did not. I decided to do it right." Soul Selector stomped
over to Jesse. This was getting ridiculous. The kid needed to
move on, and hopefully not in the way Aphrodite decreed.
Soul Selector had to find somewhere safe to store Jesse until
she could be reincarnated so she could meet her soul mate in
another lifetime and pick up where they left off. They had lost
their synchronicity, but it might still be possible. And Death
could damn well help her with the synchronization, as it was all
his fault they were out of whack in the first place.

"Where'd these trees come from?" she said, noticing the
changes around her pool. "And the rocks."

Jesse looked up. "Death said I redecorated with my mind,
but it was a totally subconscious thing."

Soul Selector shuffled from foot to foot.

"I'd put it back the way I found it, but I don't know how I did it in the first place," Jesse said. "If you don't like it change it back, okay?"

Soul Selector was unhappy. "Maybe," she mumbled. Why was this girl so much better at everything than she was?

Jesse raised an eyebrow. "You've no idea how, do you?"

"Maybe I'll change it, maybe I won't. That's my business. And stop messing with my things. I leave you alone for a couple of weeks and look what happens, you refurnish." She kind of liked the trees but was damned if she would show it.

"A couple of weeks!" Jesse glanced over to Death. "Has it really been a couple of weeks?"

He shrugged. "Look in the pool and see if anything has changed."

Jesse looked. The bright hospital ward was gone, replaced by an intimate, candlelit restaurant. "It's totally changed."

"Then time has moved on," Death said.

"Hard time." Soul Selector pointed out.

Death rolled his eyes. "Hard, soft. Who cares?"

"I care," Jesse said. "I care very much. That's my soul mate down there. On a date. And I'm stuck up here with you two."

Soul Selector stiffened. "You told her she had a soul mate?" she asked Death. "You actually told her?"

"It sort of popped out." Death smoothed his shell suit with anxious hands.

"Your brain sort of popped out," she yelled. "It popped out of your toaster oven head like a poisoned waffle."

"I can't believe she's on a date." Jesse was almost falling into the water she was leaning so far forward.

"What do you mean on a date?" Soul Selector loomed over her to look. "She's supposed to die an unhappy old maid. What in Hades—" The restaurant scene left her wordless. Her nice, freakishly controlled world was spinning away from her. Nothing was as it was supposed to be.

"It's not right." Jesse echoed her own sentiment. "Who's that with her?"

"Who?" Now Death was hanging over the pool for an ogle. "What are you looking at? Oh, she's lovely, isn't she? I like her top."

"Stuff her top. They're on a date, aren't they? It's hardly a business meeting with candles and champagne." Jesse was belligerent in her distress.

"And you had to tell her this particular woman was her soul mate?" Soul Selector glared at Death. "What kind of personality disorder compels you to do these things?"

"I told you. It just popped out. Can we zoom in on that top?"

"No, we cannot zoom in on that top. This is a scrying pool not a periscope. What are you planning to do? Torpedo the waiter? I can't believe you told her."

Death sighed. "No one forgets or forgives around here. It's an emotionally unhealthy atmosphere."

"Can you at least tell me her name?" Jesse asked, still transfixed.

"No, I can't," Soul Selector snapped. "I don't know her."

"You don't know her? But she's my soul mate."

Soul Selector realized she was staring not at Norrie but at her dining companion, and not because of her nice top. The woman's soul interested her even though she was not one of Soul Selector's charges.

"Well, can we at least see her slacks?"

"No! I told you before, this is a scrying pool not a fashion supplement. Go buy a *Vogue*."

"Peevishness is an ugly look," Death said.

Soul Selector ignored him and concentrated on the restaurant. There was something about her, the woman sitting across from Norrie Maguire. Something important that she should make note of, but Soul Selector didn't know what it was, and that disturbed her more than any of Jesse's antics. She was getting a headache, something she had not experienced since… since forever. She never experienced pain. When had she ever felt anything physical?

"What do you mean you don't know her name? You have to know her name," Jesse said.

"Will you both shut up and let me think!" She massaged her temples. *One thing at a time. Try and deal with one thing at a time.* "Jesse, your soul mate is called Norullah Bernadette Therese Maguire, or Norrie for short. She's a musician, she lives in Ireland, and stop looking at her. It's against the rules."

"Strictly speaking, this is a unique situation so there are no wools," Death said.

"Oh, shut up."

"Norrie." A huge smile spread over Jesse's face. "Norrie. What a lovely name."

"I like Norrie's sense of style." Death hunched over the pool beside Jesse.

"She's wonderful, isn't she." Jesse slipped onto her stomach. Her gaze was so intent on the couple below, she barely blinked. Soul Selector frowned. Norrie's name had made Jesse even more bewitched. Her left temple throbbed. What was she doing here? This situation was skewing out of control, Aphrodite was biting at her neck, and she had no idea what to do.

"Oh, for Zeus's sake, would you all step away from MY pool? Stop looking. It is not for spying on your soul mate and definitely not for window-shopping. Get away, both of you." She shooed at them, but they refused to budge.

"She's tetchier than usual today," Jesse said.

"The goddess of love tore her a new buttonhole." Death wiggled down beside Jesse and got more comfortable. "This place looks posh. What's on the menu?"

They were completely ignoring her. Soul Selector dithered near their prone bodies, then, feeling stupid, she stomped off to stretch out on the grass several yards away. She was unsure what to do next, and she hadn't the energy to deal with Death's and Jesse's obstinacy right now. It was probably better they were harmlessly occupied ogling in the pool. It gave her time to think, if only her head would stop throbbing.

Who was that woman with Norrie? And why did her soul catch Soul Selector's attention like that? Soul Selector was definite the woman was not one of her souls. The look and vibration was all wrong, and yet…What was it? And why was she hurting? Her body never hurt. She never felt anything, so why was she feeling terrible now?

"Can we pull back and see what the other diners are wearing? Oh, you are good at this. I'm sure Soulie couldn't do that."

Soul Selector lay flat out and moaned in her private misery. She gave up. What was the point of anything anymore? Her self-pity was interrupted by Death who loomed over her blocking out the sky.

"Finally," she said. "The shadow of death."

"Soulie." His big, brown eyes were huge with worry. "You need to come see this."

"Leave me alone."

"Please."

"It's Soul Selector, not Soulie," she muttered, not expecting him to pay any attention.

"I need you to look at this." His wheedling was making the pain in her head worse, and she knew it wouldn't stop until Death got his way. With great effort, she climbed to her feet and followed him to the pool. She was hot and tired, and her long black robe felt cumbersome and ridiculous. It wrapped around her legs so that stalking through the prairie grass became hard work. Everything about her body itched and irritated. Something was wrong, seriously wrong.

"Look," Death whispered, pointing toward the restaurant scene. Soul Selector focused her tired eyes on the image.

Immediately, she was drawn to Norrie's companion. She was concentrating so hard on the woman she almost missed it.

"See?" Death breathed into her ear. He took a surreptitious peek at Jesse to make sure she hadn't overheard.

Soul Selector did see. A flaming arrow arced over the heads of the other diners and slammed in a plume of fire into the table between the young women. It spat and fizzled out. They didn't see it. The blackened, burned out shaft of an earlier arrow also lay on the charred tablecloth. Soul Selector took a quick glance at Jesse. She was totally oblivious. She couldn't see the celestial archery any more than the two at the table did. Which was a mercy. How could she explain any of this to Jesse when she had no idea what Eros was up to? How dare he fire love arrows at her charge. What in Hades was the little runt thinking?

"Why is he doing that?" Death asked, voicing her own question. "Does Aphwodite know?"

"If not then I'm damned well going to tell her." Soul Selector was furious. Another hail of fiery arrows sailed across the restaurant. Hundreds of them rained down like molten raindrops on the young women. Arrows pierced their bodies until their flesh scorched and split. Their clothes lay in cinders around their feet. Their hair burst into flames, and the women laughed. They sipped wine and discussed the menu unaware of the firestorm engulfing them.

Soul Selector sat in shock. It was a hellish, unprecedented, maelstrom.

"In the name of all the gods!" Death was aghast. "Even the Norse ones."

"They're not hitting their hearts," Soul Selector said.

"What?"

"The arrows. They're not hitting their hearts."

It was true. Eros's arrows flew in their hundreds until the entire restaurant was a furnace. The table linen ignited. The chairs, the carpet, other diners, everything burned. Central to it all, the women sat tête-à-tête, blazing like hilltop beacons in a field of fire, and still not one arrow had hit its target and pierced a heart.

"He's missed them every time." Soul Selector was mystified.

"But Ewos can't miss," Death said. "He's the messenger of love. How can he miss?"

"Because they're mine!" Soul Selector slapped her chest. "They're protected. He couldn't hit them if we nailed them to a barn," she said, awed by the idea. "It's as if their hearts are armor-plated."

"Both of them? I thought only one soul was yours?"

Soul Selector didn't answer him. She had no answer. She had no idea what was going on.

CHAPTER TWENTY-FIVE

The *Lon Dubh* was famous for its fish. Local trawlers landed their catch at Killybegs Harbor at dawn, and the best was on the *Lon Dubh* menu that evening. Norrie was pleased she had managed to book a table at such short notice though she felt a pang of guilt that her fame had most likely enabled it. It was worth it though, selling out her celebrity ass to see the look of pleasure on Loa's face when they were shown to a table in a quiet corner. Candlelight silvered the wine glasses and splashed the white linen with a soft romantic glow. The waiter took their coats leaving them to peruse a pair of enormous menus.

"This place is fantastic." Loa kept peeping over her menu to check out the rest of the restaurant. Norrie began to worry she had overdone it, but she wanted to treat Loa, and this was the best restaurant for miles. She considered this their third date. After the private piano recital, they had met again a few days later. Their follow-up date was a long walk on the beach and a pub lunch. This dinner date was more formal, but Norrie wanted it to be special. Slowly, they were declaring their hands though neither had much of a poker face to begin with. It was obvious the attraction was there. The question was did they want to go along with it? Norrie could feel a heat rising between them. Her face felt hot, and Loa's eyes had a sharp, diamond edged sparkle. They were both giddy and they hadn't even ordered wine yet.

"Why did you come back to Ireland?" Loa asked her once they had made their wine selection and placed their food orders with the waiter. "I thought America was the heart of the music industry. Wasn't it best to stay in the thick of it?"

"I've paid my regards to Broadway," Norrie said, smiling. "I loved America, but once I'd made my name as a songwriter rather than a performer, I couldn't wait to get back home. I can write music anywhere in the world so why not on my own doorstep?"

"I'd love to live in America, if only for a little while."

"It is a wonderfully diverse country, but I found I missed my family more than I expected. And I love Donegal. It stimulates me. The landscape suits me. It kindles my creativity." Norrie played with the stem of her wine glass. "I've done some of my best work here. I think I need the solitude." This was an old conversation for her. She had gone over this ground many, many times, and her answers were almost rehearsed. Secretly, she hoped Loa would lead them into more personal territory. Surely by the third date that was to be expected.

"Maybe America had too many distractions." Loa's switch in tense caught Norrie's ear. In certain magazines, sleazy gossip rags more like, it had been intimated she'd had a string of girlfriends. All nonsense really. There'd have to be more than twenty-four hours in a day to do all the sleeping around she'd been accused of.

"America had maybe two long-term distractions," she answered honestly. "But they didn't work out. The last one came so close it hurt, and I ran back home to cry myself out." She held Loa's gaze as she spoke. Those beautiful, expressive, caramel-colored eyes would never grow old on her; she knew that much already. Hope and excitement fluttered inside her. If they chose to have an affair, it would be a big one. All the ingredients were there for one hell of a love cake.

"I know what you mean," Loa said. "But I'm an incurable romantic, and I never seem to learn. I blame Disney. When I was a little girl, I wanted to fall in love forever, but not necessarily with the prince."

"Fairy tales did it for me." Norrie laughed. Was it her imagination or were the candles glowing brighter? They seemed to be giving off a steady stream of heat. Loa looked hot and flustered, discreetly dabbing her face with a napkin. Norrie was beginning to regret ordering the paprika crusted salmon; she was overheated enough.

"Same thing," Loa said. "Disney homogenizes everything."

"So we're brainwashed into happy ever afters from year dot. What a waste. They should brainwash kids into sensible stuff like education."

"Says the woman who's made her fortune from love songs." Loa laughed at her. Their food arrived, but the conversation continued. The heat built, skin glowed, and eyes glittered. A tendril of Loa's hair slipped from behind her ear. They were burning up, and the looks they exchanged grew hotter and hotter.

"Is your car outside?" Norrie asked. They were saying good night at the restaurant doorway.

"I took a taxi."

"Then I'll give you a lift home," she said, secretly delighted. She wanted this night to go somewhere, and she was more than happy to be in the driver's seat.

Outside, the heat of the restaurant still clung to them. The night breeze was surprisingly balmy for the time of year making them shrug off their coats and stash them on the backseat. Loa slid into the passenger side, fanning herself with her purse.

"Boy, but it was hot in there. Was the central heating on or what? I was melting in my seat."

Norrie grinned. She'd been melting in her seat too, but not necessarily from the heat. She leaned over and kissed Loa on the mouth. Loa started for a split second, then her mouth softened and she moved into the kiss. Norrie half expected Loa to withdraw from the kiss, hopefully excited and wanting more. Then Norrie would offer to drive them both back to her place to continue their lovemaking in comfort. It was asking for trouble making out in the car park like a couple of horny teenagers, even if it was well past midnight and the place half empty. Loa's hands moved to her thighs. Norrie hadn't expected that. Loa's fingers left trails of fire across her skin.

"I've got to get you home," she whispered against her lips.

"Your place is closer," Loa murmured into her mouth.

"That's what I meant." Her words were lost in a moan. She slid her hand into Loa's blouse and under the lace cup of her brassiere. The nipple hardened under her fingertips. She pinched it and Loa growled so deep and rich that Norrie's insides liquefied. This was passion well out of her control, out of both their control. She was practically devouring Loa on her front car seats. She could feel the heat rolling off Loa's body and smell the warm spice of her skin. She ran her tongue along her neck and began nibbling at her ear.

With a throaty moan, Loa spilled her over onto her back and covered her. Norrie buried her fingers in the silken curls that tumbled over Loa's shoulders and spilled against her face while Loa stroked the bareness of her shoulder and up her arm to her wrist where she kissed the hammering pulse. Then she lowered her head and nuzzled the sensitive spot below Norrie's ear, moving to the hollow of her throat, up to her eyebrow, and trailing little kisses into her hairline. The teasing stopped when Norrie grabbed Loa, a hand either side of her face, and kissed her hard, sucking on her full lower lip. Norrie lapped her up, the scent, texture, heat of her mouth and tongue. Tasting until her own tongue burned.

Norrie moaned, her fingers playing with hair as heavy and black as the night surrounding them. She twisted the hair into hungry fistfuls, and wrapped her arms and legs around Loa.

They were not gentle. They were hungry for each other. Their kisses were urgent, their hands greedy. Loa pulled aside Norrie's underwear. She could hear it rip. Then Loa was plunging into her, and she was cresting to meet her and closing tightly around her. She tore at Loa's blouse ripping buttons off and exposing the tantalizing lace and the soft flesh spilling from it.

Norrie pushed the lace aside, and Loa's breasts spilled into her hands. Loa moaned and drove faster and harder at Norrie's sex, pushing her dangerously close to the edge. Norrie dug her nails into the soft flesh and squeezed. She lifted her head to nuzzle Loa's breasts, lapping at her nipples with broad strokes of her tongue until she felt her tremble with her own need. Loa's scent was strong; she had paced herself to Norrie's own needs. Norrie pushed once, twice, hard against her hand and exploded. Her body jerked in the tight confines of the car. She moaned quietly into the expensive leather both sated and annoyed that she had not pleasured Loa to the same degree.

"Oh my God," she said when she finally sucked in enough air.

Loa was upright trying to rebutton her mauled blouse and smiling as if she'd won the lottery.

"You're a beast." Norrie struggled to pull down her dress with shaking hands. "A sneaky, sexy beast."

"I don't know what came over me." Loa laughed. "I'm not usually so voracious. I swear it was like I was on fire or something."

Loa tried to fix her hair with shaking hands, and Norrie reached over to playfully tug a runaway tendril. "I felt I was going to explode, so I damn well did. Even the car is all steamed up." She rubbed a circle on the window and looked out. Luckily, their antics had not been noticed. "Let's get out of here."

She put the key in the ignition and started the motor.

"Would you like to come back for coffee?" she asked, just in case Loa had changed her mind.

She hadn't.

Norrie pulled out of the restaurant car park and turned for home. In her rearview mirror she could swear there were sparks flying from the *Lon Dubh's* chimneys. Then they turned a bend in the road, and Loa's hand was on her knee, and she forgot all about it.

CHAPTER TWENTY-SIX

What the hell is going on?" Soul Selector's angry pacing swished a yard-wide furrow. Her cloak swathed through the grass like a scythe.

"I don't know. I can't look once people get naked." Death turned his blushing face away.

"I'm surprised. I thought this would be the moment you stole their clothes."

"Sarcasm is a weak substitute for poor conversational skills." He sniffed. "Even monkeys do sarcasm. They display their genitalia."

"How would you know? You'd be too busy looking the other way."

"You're doing it again."

"Would you two stop bickering and help me?" Jesse rubbed her eyes dry. She had been quietly crying. "I need to get down there. Norrie is with the wrong person, and it's killing me, except you two idiots have already seen to that."

"Here we go again," Death muttered under his breath.

"I'm so sorry to upset you by wanting to live," Jesse yelled at them. "I want to be down there with her, and because of you I can't. It hurts; it actually hurts." She turned away. "It hurts like hell, and you just don't get it."

Soul Selector quietly indicated for Death to follow her. They moved a few steps out of Jesse's hearing.

"I feel so bad for her, Soulie," he said. "It can't be nice to see the love of your life sleeping with someone else."

"Don't feel bad about that." Soul Selector nodded at the pool and the images of Norrie and Loa between the sheets. "Feel bad that Aphrodite wants her tipped."

"Tipped?"

"Dumped. Tipped out with the trash."

Death gasped. "Not the slush pile!"

Soul Selector nodded. "The slush pile of souls."

"But she's a soul mate! She can't be slushied. She has a destiny, a job to do, love to make, a universe to save."

"Exactly what I said, only I said it better. Aphrodite wouldn't hear of it. She says the kid has to go."

"No. You can't do it, Soulie."

"Well, technically, I don't do it. You do." She gave him a stern look. He recoiled.

"I can't do that to her," he said. "I hate taking out the twash, even for defective souls. The slush pile scares me."

Soul Selector shrugged. "Not my problem."

"But I can't, Soulie. I just can't."

"Then you'll have to help me come up with another plan."

"What plan?" Death said, his eyes slick with suspicion. "Have you just bamboozled me?"

"Easily. But apparently, death-defying dogs bamboozle you so I'm not going to brag about it. First we need to take her—Where is she?" Soul Selector looked around her, her panic growing by the second. Jesse was gone.

"She's very good at teleporting." Death did his own three-sixty turn. "She learns fast, much faster than you ever did."

"Can we just focus on the fact she has gone?"

"Let's face it; she had little to stick awound for. She's dead, her girlfriend has another squeeze, she's stuck here with you—"

"Shut up and help me find her."

"What can I do?"

"You check out the Titan marshes, and I'll run over to Aphrodite's temple to see if she's grabbed her."

"I don't like the Titans. They pick on me."

"Do you want to go to the temple instead?"

"No. Aphwodite picks on me more."

"Then go strike a pose with the big boys."

With a sad sigh, Death dematerialized. Soul Selector walked back to the pool. She stood by its edge for one last look, as if she could somehow divine Jesse's whereabouts. It was useless. She simply hadn't the skill.

Loa Ebele came into focus. She was curled up on a settee surrounded by a million cushions, reading a book. There was a glass of wine by her elbow, and a fat ginger cat slept right on top of her feet. This was the fastest Soul Selector had ever managed to call up a vision. Had she called Loa? It was Jesse she should be concerned about, and yet she found herself settling on the grassy bank and leaning back against one of Jesse's jacaranda trees. The purple blossoms hung over her head, and blue jays, no doubt Jesse's latest addition to her pool, sang in the higher branches. Soul Selector sat on, steady and unblinking, fixed on the woman with the book and the cat on her feet.

There was something else she should be doing right now. Oh yes, looking for Jesse. But she was tired to the point of exhaustion. So tired she didn't really care.

Chapter Twenty-seven

Death found the first worthwhile clue. Eros was sulking in the family room at the foot of Mount Olympus. By the time Soul Selector arrived, his sulk had become a full on attitude problem. It seemed Eros lacked an audience to whine at. Now he had the two of them so he let rip.

"Fucking Valentine cards and girly kitsch, that's all I am. Look at that fat bastard Ares. War and mayhem everywhere and he won't move his ass to deal with it. He's not doing his job, man. I'm the one with the arrows. I should be a war god not some sappy kissogram."

"Ewos! That's your father you're talking about." Death was appalled.

"Fuck him."

Death gave a prissy little gasp. "He's been in a mood all day," he told Soul Selector.

Soul Selector wasn't surprised at Eros's outburst. The Olympian Gods were trash. There was not one pleasant personality between them, and Death fell for it every time. He was always looking for the good in people so he could whisk them away to a nicer yonderland. If gods could lie down and die then it would be straight to the slush pile with this lot, and she would drag them there by the heels herself! This happy little fantasy reminded her of Jesse's fate if she didn't find the kid as soon as possible. The afterlife was no place for her to be wandering around lost. Gods were not always the nicest people.

"What were you doing firing arrows at my soul mate?" she said. If the little snot knew anything, she'd wring it out of him with her bare hands. "My people are out of bounds to the gods. You can fuck around with everyone else but not my lot."

"And fuck you, too." Eros was as scintillating as ever. Aphrodite or Ares, it was hard to say which obnoxious parent he took after the most. Death clucked his tongue. All the swearing was distressing him. He hated unpleasantness; for him, everything had to be cheesecake shaped with cream pies on top. Soul Selector could see he'd be next to useless with this interrogation.

"Tell me what you were up to or you'll be pulling arrows out of more than your quiver." She put on her best intimidating look and Eros deflated like the voided bladder he was.

"Mom made me. She said to shoot 'em up. She wants them to fall in love." Then he turned toxic again and said, "Ask her, not me. Like I give a shit about any of it."

"Considering you failed after about a million shots, I'd say your mom's pretty miffed with you," Death said. He hit his mark. "Is that why you're hiding here, hurting on the inside?"

Eros reddened. Aphrodite must have already torn a scab off her spotty teenager.

"That was your fault, not mine," he shouted at Soul Selector. "I can't touch your shitty old soul mates' hearts, and I don't want to either. I wouldn't waste an arrow on your losers."

"You wasted hundreds of them, you dweeb. I could see you. I have a scrying pool, remember?" Soul Selector tapped her forehead to underline his stupidity. "Loser." It was childish, but it was fun.

Eros flipped her the bird and dematerialized. His adieu of, "Fuck you all," evaporating in the clement afternoon air.

"Pestiferous little shit."

"Sh!" Death even held a finger to his lips and looked around with huge, nervous eyes. "This place could be bugged."

"It is. It's full of divine cockroaches. Now we need to go see Aphrodite and find out why she tried to ping my people. And we still need to find Jesse." Her headache was returning worse than ever, and again she wondered at this new phenomenon. She also noted she had begun to bite her fingernails. She scraped the ragged edges against the ball of her thumb in morbid fascination. Her body was breaking down and had been since the moment Jesse Colvin appeared dead on the doorstep.

"She wasn't at the Titan marshes," Death said glumly.

"Rough, eh?"

"They said my hair was stupid."

"The agony." Soul Selector was disinterested in whatever torture the Titans had heaped upon Death's dainty shoulders. "Where could she be? If you were wandering the Elysian Fields as a prematurely deceased teenager, where would you go? It's not as if we have a mall."

"I know." Death sighed heavily. "Why do all the big corporate retailers have to go to hell? We have no decent shopping here."

"Think, man. Where would she go?"

"I don't think she'd go anywhere. I think she'd have been picked up by now. She's too obvious. Too out of place."

"Picked up?"

"By Zeus. You know what a control fweak he is. He has spies everywhere." Death looked around nervously. "Lovely god that he is," he added.

"What on earth would Zeus want with an orphaned soul mate?" Soul Selector sounded scornful, but her stomach fluttered uneasily; another new physical feeling. She was falling apart.

"That's what the Titans said, and they usually know what's going on."

"The Titans! When were you going to spill this little gem?"

"I'm telling you now, aren't I?" he said.

"When did they tell you this? I thought they pulled your stupid hair or something?" He refused to catch her eye. "You burst into tears, didn't you?" she said at last, truth dawning. "And they felt sorry for you, didn't they?" Still he refused to look at her. "So they told you stuff to shut you up." She gave a snort of derision.

"So, why can't you scwee for her, Soulie?" He stomped his cowboy booted foot. "Why do we have to go through all this unpleasantness with Ewos and the Titans?"

Soul Selector didn't want to admit that every time she went to the pool all she could summon up was the woman hanging out with Norrie, the one who wasn't even a soul mate. Somehow, she was wrapped up in this mess. Was she a trap? The bait in some elaborate game Aphrodite was playing? Each time the woman appeared in her scrying pool, Soul Selector's worries receded until she almost forgot about Jesse and Norrie. That was bad, very bad. She was close to neglecting her duties, and that was exactly what Aphrodite had accused her of. This woman's presence was a distraction. There had to be something sinister behind her appearance in Norrie's life. Soul Selector's left eye began to tic in perfect rhythm with the pulse in her temple.

"Scrying won't help if she's up here on the Celestial Plain. My pool is pointed toward the earthly sphere." It was a fudged answer, but she could see Death didn't notice. His pixie dust mind had floated off elsewhere.

"You need to go up there." Death pointed vaguely to the spiraling snow-packed peaks of Mount Olympus and Zeus's lair. He did not sound very enthusiastic.

"Me? I think you'll find it's *we*," she said.

"How long am I to be tortured? You're as bad as the Titans! Haven't I paid my debt?" He actually wrung his hands at her.

"You're to be tortured for as long as it's fun. Like the Titans, I enjoy a good laugh. *You* slaughtered my soul mate and *you* started this mess. Believe me, you are not the one suffering here." She laid it on thick. She couldn't afford to lose him, not at this point. "Jesse's suffering. *I* am suffering. I have Aphrodite pissing on my picnic blanket because she's short on manna, and it's all your doing. I was a highflyer until you showed up with your quack houses and non-dead dogs. Now I'm the cruddiest of the crud on the sole of her shoe."

"What kind of shoe?"

"Shut up. You're helping, and that's that."

Soul Selector cricked her neck and stared up to the summit of Mount Olympus. The Celestial collective gathered on the utmost peak. Somewhere up there stood the great temple where Zeus resided. He was a bored, idle god who used anything or anyone that wandered within range for entertainment. The peaks were milk white and ragged as broken teeth. The home of the gods gave out no light and no hope. No happiness emanated from it. Its crags were sculpted into scowls, its crevices gaping wounds. Birds of prey circled, and their harried cries echoed down the mountainside.

"Can you teleport us up there?" she asked Death. It took a lot of energy even for an entity such as herself to breach the divine walls of Olympus, and she didn't have it. It scared her that her energy levels were so low. Power had been slowly seeping out of her since the aches and pains arrived, lending weight to her suspicions of sabotage.

"Why? You should be able to do it easily."

"It's easier for you. Death knows no door and all that."

"That doesn't mean I pick locks. Zeus will flay us alive and then make us eat our own skin. He's done it before." Death's eyes grew large and panicked. "I heard there was this guy once with bad psoriasis and Zeus made him eat his own skin and he poisoned himself to death."

"Of course he died. He'd been flayed! Now concentrate, you idiot. We need to find Jesse and get her to a safe place. She is not going to end up in a trash can," she said. "You're the one who thinks she might be up there so you can lead the way."

"And you need to find out why Aphwodite is trying to hook up your little soul mate with a mortal." Death was kicking back. He was not going to be the only one with a task.

"Yes. That, too," she conceded. The difficult questions were piling up all around her, and they all concerned Jesse. Zeus might have the answer to at least one, her charge's whereabouts.

CHAPTER TWENTY-EIGHT

Mount Olympus hovered over the Elysian Fields the way a hungry raven hangs over a newborn lamb. The more she thought about it the more Soul Selector was convinced Death was right. A strange, unattached soul like Jesse would be plucked out of the fields like the dewy eye out of a baby lamb. Zeus had to have her. She'd rather it was Zeus. He was more likely to stick to the rules than any of the other gods, demigods, and monstrosities that wandered the Fields, if only because he made the damned rules.

"Ah. You've arrived for your audience." The great god's chief administrative nymph, Thalia, greeted them with approval and an armful of papers.

"That was quick." Soul Selector was astounded; she'd only completed the forms five and a half years ago.

"You were fast-tracked."

"Oh? Why?"

"Special dispensation. Your case caught his attention." Thalia nodded toward a huge granite throne at the end of a humongous hall. "You were designated as a HI, or High Interest. Zeus likes his highs." She made it sound as if high interest was not a good thing.

Like Aphrodite's temple, the wind roared through Zeus's great hall at an uncomfortable velocity. It was basically a wind tunnel. Thalia clung to her clipboard as papers tried to twist out of her grasp. Sleek marble columns soared into the night sky and plunged into the Milky Way. The intended effect being that they actually supported it. A prime example of Zeus's PR.

Starlight lit the temple like a celestial chandelier. It shone with a hard crystalline light that hurt the eyes of the undivine. Everything lit up flat and hard edged so that shadows became eerie, fathomless places. While the soft glow of the Galaxy pulsed all around it, the temple itself was a stark place of contrasts.

Soul Selector squinted. She was far from divine and the light hurt. The beginning of another headache began to brew. On top of the nagging pain came the nagging worry that something was awry. She had never had an audience with Zeus before. He was one of those gods she avoided. Okay, so she tried to avoid them all, though she was beholden to report to Aphrodite once in a while, as she was the CEO of her department. Everyone knew if you caught Zeus's eye there was always a chore involved. He loved to invent work for others. Gargantuan work. Tasks and quests and epic adventures that killed, and maimed, and caused all sorts of psychological damage while he sat back and spectated as if he were in some amphitheater.

She could see him at the far end of the great hall. His presence was so overpowering it saturated the atmosphere like dew. Every atom of him pressed upon the mind until there was room for little else. Zeus had the atypical god-look. He was a big, hulking man with a long white beard. Draped in a toga of snow white finery, he looked well-groomed and wise. His gaze managed to be all knowing even as it bubbled with curiosity. It was his mouth that betrayed him; it was wet, weak, and self-indulgent.

"Ah, the Soul Selector is here." His voice boomed across the acres of hall. It felt as if the air was rippling around her. He motioned for her to step forward. Soul Selector took one step on the long journey to his throne and found herself directly before him. It was disconcerting the way his temple bent space. She collected herself and bowed her knee with great dignity. Not knowing his mood, it was best to stick to the strictest protocol.

"Arise, Soul Selector." He sounded relaxed and gleeful. Not necessarily a good thing. Zeus's gleefulness usually came at a cost.

"My lord," she muttered and stood upright.

"I think I have something of yours. Well, a fraction of it, at least." He gestured to his right and Jesse materialized. She looked confused and a little intimidated. "Well?" He looked at Soul Selector with interest.

"This is Jesse, my lord. She is a soul mate."

"I can see that. But what is she doing running about my Elysian Fields? That is not the place for soul mates. And where is her other half? There's never one of these things without another one nearby." He could have been talking about mice.

"Um. Down on earth, my lord," Soul Selector tried to placate. "You see, there was a little complication."

Zeus clicked his fingers and Death appeared beside her. He had made an extra effort in that he now wore a white tuxedo, but looked like he wanted to be anywhere else, even the Titan marshes.

"A complication?" Zeus said, looking at Death expectantly.

"She was not on my list," Death mumbled into his chest.

"And yet she managed to die." Zeus raised a snowy white eyebrow.

"Sorry. I've no idea how it happened."

"Indeed. Neither have I, and that's why I am fascinated. What do you plan to do with her?" For a god who assumed he already knew all the answers, asking a question was a sure sign of trouble. Soul Selector shifted uncomfortably.

"She's to be recycled." The imperious voice rang out seconds before the Goddess of Love popped out of the ether to stand before them. Aphrodite appeared before Zeus, but sensibly one step below the dais his throne rested on. She might be arrogant, but she wasn't stupid.

"Recycled? I see." It was obvious Zeus didn't. A bad sign, it meant he would burrow his aquiline nose in even deeper.

"Slushied! She's to be slushied. Slushied!" Death squeaked, hurling himself toward the edge of hysteria. It had obviously been a long day for him. Soul Selector shrunk back. Aphrodite would be furious at her plans being exposed before her father. Every fault line in the earth's crust would be ground to pulp, and the planet would go splat.

"Slushied?" Zeus echoed. Death nodded his head like a manic puppet. Aphrodite seethed, her face a sullen mask of malice.

"Is this true, daughter dear?" Zeus turned to her.

Aphrodite shrugged. "A lone soul mate is no use to me. I need the manna-loaded ones. I want to dissolve this one and move on. Time is manna."

Zeus seemed to agree with this logic.

"Hang on," Jesse spoke up. There was a heartbeat of icy silence throughout the hall. Mortal souls like Jesse did not speak out in the hallowed halls of Olympus. Human souls were more or less invisible; they were tiny, inconsequential things to the workings of the gods. Zeus brightened as if clouds had lifted to reveal a wonderful summer day. He was totally enthralled by the unfolding drama. Soul Selector's stomach cramped. Zeus was delighted with the distraction Jesse was providing. The last thing she wanted was for Jesse to become his next hobby. Zeus had a habit of losing interest in his toys, abandoning them at the most inopportune moments. Being his protégée was not an enviable position.

"Hang on," Jesse repeated. "I'm not alone. I can see my soul mate in the scrying pool."

Soul Selector winced. Aphrodite threw her a venomous look, and Zeus gave her a surprised but calculating one. She realized he thought she'd been clever letting Jesse use the pool. Her left eye twitched, and she was mortified. Zeus thought she was winking at him. He winked back.

"You can actually see your other half?" Zeus asked Jesse. Soul Selector noted glumly that after two millennia of taking hardly any interest in humanity, Zeus was suddenly riveted to this particular specimen.

"She's looking for me," Jesse told him. "Though she doesn't know she's doing that. But I do. I can see her down there waiting for me. And if you allow me to be destroyed, then she'll be waiting forever and that's not fair."

"It is not." Zeus was indulging her, and that wasn't good either. "Up here we like stories where love conquers all."

Lying old goat. Soul Selector could see blood all over the walls, and if she had any to bleed out, there was no doubt it would be hers.

"This is *my* jurisdiction," Aphrodite said. She was getting angrier by the second but trying to keep it in check. "It's up to me to decide what to do here, and I need the floor cleared. There are too many loose ends. We need manna not drama."

"Aren't you intrigued she can see her soul mate through the scrying pool?" Zeus asked her.

"Yes. That intrigues me a lot." She shot a glance at Soul Selector who did not like the gleam in the goddess's eye at all. It did not bode well. She began rehearsing an apology for allowing Jesse to get anywhere near her pool.

"Nevertheless," Aphrodite continued, "she belongs to my department, and I demand her to be handed over." The other gods knew what a pain in the ass Zeus's meddling could be, and Aphrodite was no exception.

"But I filled out forms." Soul Selector was shocked to hear her own voice. She sounded like a suicidal sheep bleating in the wilderness. Why, when she'd had no intention of saying a word, was she speaking up now? It was madness. "There are rules," she added, shocking herself further. Aphrodite did not look happy.

"Yes. Wools!" Death piped up over her shoulder. She could hear the tip tapping of his spats as he wedged in behind her out of sight.

Zeus settled more comfortably into his throne. He wasn't going anywhere soon. It was too late now. He was fully immersed in the little theater playing out before him. Soul Selector would have to follow through with whatever he decided. This was no longer Aphrodite's call, which might be the only thing in Jesse's favor.

"Ah, the rules." Zeus's booming voice was leaden with false gravitas. His eyes glittered with whimsy. "We need to think about those."

Aphrodite shifted. It was the slightest of movements but enough for Soul Selector to know she was furious. It was always bad news when Zeus's will was foisted upon another department, but he had the power to do it if he chose to.

"This soul has arrived unscheduled onto the Celestial Plains." Aphrodite took one more try at derailing him. "She has somehow warped her earthly path and is now useless." She shrugged as casually as she could though her eyes were slick with anger. "It happens. Once in a while we get a dud." She glared at Soul Selector to clarify just who the dud was.

"But not that often." Death's voice came out from under Soul Selector's armpit. "Jesse's an anomaly." He sounded proud of her.

"And you want to eradicate her because she's an anomaly?" Zeus asked Aphrodite.

"It's the purest solution." She sneakily appealed to his sense of order. He had a whole universe to keep in line, after all. Anomalies should be the last thing he needed.

"But the paperwork," Soul Selector protested. Why couldn't she just shut up?

Jesse spoke over her. "I didn't ask to be brought to the Celestial Plains. I was happy with my earthly path until it was ripped out from under me. I want to go back. I want to be with my soul mate."

"She can't go back. Even if we were to reincarnate her, she'd be out of sync with her soul mate. They would never meet up. Best to cut our losses and start again." Aphrodite addressed Zeus, ignoring Jesse.

"But we have wools!" Despite his fear, Death emerged from behind her, hanging in there like a trembling terrier. Soul Selector admitted some grudging admiration for his lemming-like advance.

"Yes. We have to abide by the rules." She backed him up. He was her only ally. Zeus wrote the rules, so it made sense he'd have to abide by them, too, and make everyone else do the same.

"This is an extraordinary situation." Aphrodite hit back.

"Then it demands an extraordinary solution." Jesse was no pushover. She was fighting back.

It was becoming a tug-of-war for Jesse's soul. Soul Selector was unsure why Aphrodite was so adamant to annihilate her. Okay, so singular soul mates were not the norm, but surely there was somewhere they could stick her until the right time for reincarnation came along. Maybe they could sync her and her soul mate at some future date? Then they could get on with making manna and everyone would be happy.

"Has this ever happened before?" Soul Selector asked, remembering Aphrodite's jibe that she had messed up previously. She knew she hadn't. But if the Celestial collective had come across prematurely deceased souls before, how had they dealt with them? Surely this couldn't be an unprecedented event.

Aphrodite went rigid.

"It can happen, but not that often," Zeus answered in a vague way that nevertheless brooked no further inquiry. He turned back to Jesse. "So what shall we do about you, my little lost soul?"

"I want to go back," she answered immediately.

"No, she can't," Aphrodite said, her patience spent. "I'm putting my departmental seal on this."

"What did we do last time we had a rogue soul? Refresh my memory." Zeus carried on as if she hadn't spoken, and turned to his administrator.

Thalia, who had been avidly listening to everything, gripped her clipboard and leaped into action. "We gave them the gift of time, my lord."

"What? A watch?" Sometimes Zeus betrayed what an old fool he really was.

"Time in itself, my lord." Thalia bowed her head to hide a derisive smile. Soul Selector caught it and was pleased she wasn't the only one to see through the trumped up godhead. "If the errant soul has eaten anything in the celestial realm then they can stay a designated time," Thalia said. "That's what we usually do."

"Like Persephone?" Zeus asked.

"Sort of like Persephone," Thalia said.

"Well?" Zeus turned to Soul Selector. "Has she? Surely you gave her something from the orchard of Oblivion? That would be the decent thing to do."

"I knew it!" Jesse said. "Obis, my ass."

Soul Selector scowled at her, more to cover up her own discomfort than anything. Jesse had not eaten anything from the orchard. She had been too stubborn to, and now they were stuffed. She threw Jesse a baleful look. Jesse stared back in growing alarm, obviously thinking the same thing. They'd fucked up.

"Well?" Zeus repeated.

"She ate grass," Death blurted out. Everyone looked at him and he blushed.

"Grass? Like a cow?" Zeus frowned. His impatience with the turn in the conversation was evident. "You made her eat grass?" He glared at Soul Selector. Jesse had become a firm favorite.

"No. Grass stalks, like a bluegrass singer." Death mimed chewing a stalk of grass.

"Ah." Zeus liked this idea. "That counts."

"No, it doesn't," Aphrodite said.

"Yes, it does," he boomed and everyone shut up. He turned to Jesse. "How much grass did you eat, dear?"

Jesse looked disconcerted. "One or two." She shrugged. "It's not the kind of thing you count." Then realizing it could be important, she added, "But I chewed them for a long time and they were very nice." It was the right answer.

"I see." Zeus pretended to mull this over, though it was obvious to all gathered that he'd already made his mind up. Thalia was already writing up a notice on her clipboard.

"One hard time week," he declared, focusing on Soul Selector, "to restore your soul mate to where she needs to be." He smiled, turning benevolently to Jesse. "And if you fail then Aphrodite can do as she wishes."

"One week!" Soul Selector said. Seven hard time days was a tight deadline.

Zeus rose from his throne. He had bestowed his mighty wisdom and now announced his need for a nap. Death stood by blinking liking an owl, uncertain if what had happened was a good or bad thing, and Aphrodite vanished in a puff of discontent that left a stale smell. Only Jesse looked relieved.

"Follow me, please." Thalia shooed them toward the exit. Soul Selector could hardly wait to go through it.

Chapter Twenty-nine

"Well, that sucked. What use is seven hard days in a place like this? Zeus basically gave us as long as he takes to blow his nose to save her." Soul Selector grumped.

"And Aphwodite was mean," Death said. "Why does she hate Jesse so much?"

"No idea, but she's gunning for her." Soul Selector now had another big problem. Aphrodite knew about her blunders with Jesse, like the pool and the screw-up at the orchard. It made her feel vulnerable. Aphrodite was not a forgiving boss. And to add to the mess, she had inadvertently exposed Aphrodite's plans to Zeus and his meddling ways. That would never be forgiven.

"I thought Ewos was going to wet himself," Death said happily. Their vendetta was well and truly forged.

"Eros was there?" This surprised Soul Selector. She hadn't seen him.

"He was skulking near the back. I only noticed because I was trying to skulk, too."

"Why did you think he'd wet himself?"

"I could see his overactive bladder palpitating before my eyes." He gave a mock shudder. "He was a bag of nerves. Maybe he's worried we'll mention he was shooting at your soul mate to Zeus?"

Soul Selector shook her head. An audience before Zeus was not the place to air that particular grievance. That could wait until the inevitable showdown with Aphrodite. It might give her a little leverage with the goddess.

"Where did he go?" she asked. "I suppose he ran off after his mother?"

"No," Death said. "He went out that way." He pointed to an arched gateway near the back. It was shrouded in swirling gray mist, which meant it was low-level security.

Soul Selector went over for a closer look. "This is easy for you to break through," she said.

"No, it isn't," Death said. "I need a security clearance and—" Soul Selector placed a hand on his back and shoved him through, following directly on his heels. They were in a narrow dark corridor.

"Soulie! We'll get in twouble."

"Haven't you noticed? We're already in twoub—trouble." She peered into the mire.

"You first." Death squeezed back in behind her and nudged her gently but firmly forward.

The light was faint, and strands of phosphorus trailed through it like fairy lights. This was a residue of Eros's divinity. The light trickled from his minuscule wings in a confetti of glitter that sparkled in the gloom. All the gods left phosphorescent traces with various degrees of splendor. The traces were only noticeable in the dark. Some gods blazed like comets and some glowed as subtle as gemstones. This trace was dim because Eros was a twat. Even so, Soul Selector found she could follow it a few cautious steps at a time. The corridor twisted left then right then to the left again. Every few yards, other passages opened up on either side. Only the trickle of light from Eros's wings guided them.

"It's like a maze," Death whispered. Soul Selector ignored him concentrating on the faint light ahead of them.

"If we meet the Minotaw I'm going to scweem," he said.

"What are you afraid of? You're Death for heaven's sake."

"That doesn't mean I'm bwave. My nerves are shredded, Soulie."

"Sh!"

"What! What is it? A Minotaw?" Death squeaked in her ear. His cold fingers clutched at her arm until it hurt.

"No! It's not a Minotaur. I just want you to stop talking," She shook her arm free. "Hell and damnation!" she cried. Eros had moved too far ahead and his trail had dissipated. They were lost in the darkness

"It is a Minotaw. I knew it!" Death screamed.

"No, it isn't. We've lost him."

"Who?"

"Eros. Who else are we following?"

"I can see him."

"You can? How?"

"Same as 'no door can stop me.' It's a death thing." He shrugged. "He's up ahead to the left. Ooh, I can see an exit, Soulie."

"Well, seeing as no door can stop you..." Again, Soul Selector pushed him to the fore. He timidly approached a small wooden door at the end of the corridor where he stopped short and turned back to her.

"Soulie, what if there weally is a Minotaw?"

Soul Selector sighed and pushed the door open. It was surprisingly heavy for its size and opened slowly. Immediately, the air in the corridor changed. It became hotter, desert hot. A dry wind blew in their faces and stung their eyes. The door swung fully open, and they stood on the edge of an arid landscape where the sky was an ugly tangerine color hung with a blood red sun. The dirt beneath their feet was dry and lime green. The surrounding rocks and boulders were lumpy, molten things in darker shades of green. They sat like huge misshapen toads in the bizarre desertscape.

"How howid. Where is this place, Soulie?"

"It's one of my migraines."

"Look." Death pointed. Eros was poised on the lip of an open crevice. Though the lime green earth crumbled under his feet, he stood rigid with anger glaring downward. His features creased into a nasty scowl. He started yelling, screaming expletives. Then he stooped, picked up a rock, and threw it as hard as he could. He was screaming so loudly Soul Selector could make out most of the words. Something in the hole was "stupid," and a "loser," and was getting lots and lots of "fuck yous" heaped upon it. Then the ugly little winged gargoyle stomped off, so up his own ass he didn't even notice he'd been observed.

"What was he doing? Should we go look, Soulie?"

Already Soul Selector was on the move. Death trundled along beside her darting anxious glances left and right and trying to brush the lime green dust off his white tux. Eros had been standing on the edge of a shallow hole, nothing more than a trench in the ground. A bundle of dirty rags lay heaped at the bottom.

"What was Ewos shouting at?" Death asked, then screamed as the rags began to move. They slithered away from the sound of his voice. Soul Selector stepped back in alarm.

"I'm sorry." A muffled voice emerged from the pile of rags.

"Excuse me?" Soul Selector said.

The rags unfolded, and a tall, thin woman dressed in a tattered black robe stood upright. The edge of the hole came midway to her thigh when she stood fully erect. Her hair was long and dark and caked with dirt. Her eyes were a washed out denim color sunken in a waxen, hollowed out face. Death gasped, his gaze swinging from Soul Selector to the stranger and back.

"It's like your long lost twin!" he said. Soul Selector glared at him. "Your very dirty long lost twin."

"Who are you?" Soul Selector demanded.

"I am the Soul Selector," the newcomer said.

"You are not! I am the Soul Selector." Soul Selector thumbed her chest.

The newcomer shrugged. "There have been soul selectors since the first humans fell in love, and in doing so, discovered their souls. Soul selectors reach back to the beginning of time." She sounded far too Zen for someone who'd just had rocks and insults chucked at her head. Soul Selector was immediately suspicious.

"Goodness," Death said. "Why are you in a hole? And why was Ewos being so nasty?"

"I am a prisoner of the pit of shame." The stranger hung her head. "And Eros comes to punish me. He is a callow, senseless youth. A dullard, and I only pretend to be rebuked."

"Wait a minute. Are you suggesting I'm not the only one?" Soul Selector asked.

Death tutted in sympathy. "Ewos is a meanie." He examined the hole with interest. "I didn't know we had a pit of shame. This looks more like a hole than a pit."

"I'm not the only one?" Soul Selector asked again.

"Are you sure it's not a pit?" the stranger asked.

"No, it's definitely a hole," Death said.

"I'll have you know *I* am the *only* soul selector!"

Death let out a long sigh. "Let me introduce my fwiend. This is Soul Selector, or Soulie as we call her."

"We do not." Soul Selector drew herself up to her full height, which was unnecessary, as the other soul selector was still standing in a hole and a few feet shorter than her. "I am the Soul Selector."

"I'm Sellie," Sellie said, far too affably for someone standing knee-deep in a hole. As if aware of her situation, she tried to scrabble out of it. "I'm a soul selector, too. How do you do?"

"Let me help." Death offered a hand. "I'm Death, by the way. Nice to meet you."

"Thank you. It's been a long time since I've encountered any kindness in this place," Sellie said.

"Can we concentrate on me for a minute?" Soul Selector's exasperation showed. "I am the only soul selector."

"She's got a bit of a super ego," Death muttered to Sellie who nodded knowingly.

"More like super id," she said.

"As in idiot?" he asked with genuine interest.

"As in all principle and no pleasure."

"What do you mean you're a soul selector? There's only one. And it's me." Soul Selector was becoming more and more belligerent.

"Soulie, for goodness sake look at her," Death said. "She's the spit of you. Okay, maybe a little bit faded, and frazzled, and frayed." He picked a loose thread from Sellie's shoulder. "And less fat."

"I am not fat."

"Thank you," Sellie said and shook the dust off her cloak. "I was a soul selector. I mean, I *am* one…but I burned out." The dust rose in clouds around her.

"Burned out?" Death echoed Sellie.

Soul Selector shut up. *Burned out?* Was that what was happening to her? The weird feelings, the aches and pains—was that the start of breaking down, burning out?

"We all burn out eventually. We are not eternal creatures," Sellie said.

Soul Selector grew anxious. "How did you burn out?" she asked.

"I made Aphrodite very, very angry." Sellie sighed. "I lost a soul mate. It doesn't take much to anger her."

Death shot Soul Selector a look swimming with guilt. "Soulie lost a soul mate, too," he volunteered. She glared at him and his gaze swerved back to Sellie. "Did you turn your back for just one minute?" he asked with interest.

"Less than a minute, and poof, she was gone."

"Same here. Slippery things, soul mates. Like buttered eels." Death was full of sympathy.

"What happened to you?" Sellie asked Soul Selector. Soul Selector turned away. She did not want Sellie to see her anxiety.

"It was weally all my fault," Death said. "I took her soul mate by mistake, and now Aphwodite is mad and won't listen to weason."

"You took mine, too, all those years ago." Sellie sounded sad.

Death looked contrite. "I can't wemember. I'm weally understaffed. Sorry."

"It's okay. It was a long time ago," Sellie said. "Aphrodite gets mad when the manna store runs low."

"Manna store?" Soul Selector swung round to face her.

"There's a shop here?" Death perked up.

"I thought the stuff had no shelf life," Soul Selector said. "I thought it had to be used more or less at once?"

"Oh no. She has tons of it. Stacks and stacks. It's stored in a secret room at the rear of her temple. Right behind her throne. She sits on it like a broody hen."

"Why on earth does she do that?" Soul Selector said, mostly talking to herself.

"I'm sure it's against the wools." Death tutted.

"Does Zeus know she's stockpiling?" Soul Selector asked Sellie.

"No idea, but I guess not."

"So why is she blaming you for a shortage when she has piles of the stuff? And why do we have to pulp Jesse?" Death asked.

"Who's Jesse?" Sellie asked.

"She's the stowaway soul mate," Death said.

"She landed in the Elysian Fields," Soul Selector said.

Sellie tutted sympathetically. "It's nice you managed to keep Jesse with you. When does she go up for reincarnation?"

"She doesn't. She's headed for the slush pile if we can't squeeze her in somewhere," Soul Selector said.

Sellie looked shocked.

"Aphwodite is demanding it, but Zeus gave us a few days to come up with a plan," Death butted in.

"And have you a plan?" Sellie asked Soul Selector.

"No," Death continued eagerly. "She's got no idea what to do. She's clueless." He flung his hands in the air to show the hopelessness of her situation.

She scowled at him. "I have a few ideas."

"What ideas?" he asked.

"What happened to your soul mate?" Soul Selector ignored him and directed her question to Sellie. She was loath to ask her anything, but she needed to know. Any information might prove useful.

Sellie looked contrite. "I never met her. Aphrodite whisked her away and told Eros to lock me up. Hence the pit of shame." She looked glumly at the hole.

"There is no pit of shame on the Elysian Fields," Soul Selector said. "It's a hole, that's all. A hole in the ground you chose to lie in for heaven only knows how long. It's not a celestial prison. It's a self-made one." She spoke harshly and with relish.

Sellie looked dejected. "He told me it was the pit of shame and I had to sit in it until I was allowed out."

Soul Selector rolled her eyes while Death showed genuine sympathy. "Ewos would do something like that," he said. "He's a nasty, wude boy."

"What shall I do?" Sellie asked. She looked lost now that she stepped out of her pit.

"Walk away," Soul Selector said. "He has no power over you. He's nothing more than chocolate box decor."

"Where will I walk away to?"

Soul Selector was disinterested. "Anywhere you want."

"Come along with us," Death piped up "We're on a quest. Zeus says we have seven days to help Jesse."

"A quest set by Zeus?" Sellie said. "To save Jesse? How exciting."

"I know," Death said. He was nearly breathless with excitement. Soul Selector glared at him. She did not share his sudden enthusiasm.

"Now hang on a minute—"

"Soulie needs all the help she can get," Death continued his rant.

"No, I don't"

"I'd love to help!" A delighted smile spread over Sellie's sunken face transforming her momentarily into a younger, happier version of herself.

"You can't. There are rules," Soul Selector said.

"Not for a quest," Death helpfully corrected her. "You're onboard, Sellie." He clapped his hands. "Isn't it great, Soulie? We have an expert on our team."

"We don't need another soul selector. And we don't need an expert in sitting in a hole like a big fat rabbit."

"Soulie." Death sounded shocked. "That's not fair. Aphwodite was behind that."

"I am not a rabbit. I'm a soul selector and I want to help." Sellie looked sadder than ever.

"And so you shall," Death assured her. "So she shall, Soulie, or else you're on your own. I have more than made up for my mistake. I will leave this quest if I have to."

"Listen to yourself," she said. "Since when did you become Sir Lancelot?"

But there was a new determination to his voice that made her think twice. She didn't want Death to leave. Not that she was dependent on him, she was never that, but she didn't want to carry Jesse alone. The Jesse situation overwhelmed her. She looked across at Sellie, the burned out version of herself. Her face was sallow with hollowed out cheeks and sad, red-rimmed eyes. For someone who had lain down in a hole for millennia, she looked exhausted. Her hair and clothes were filthy. There was a large bruise forming on her forearm, probably from protecting herself against Eros's stoning. He was such a little shit.

Something inside her shifted. It was not sympathy and it was not anger. She wanted Death to hang around. He was useful and she sort of liked him, and after all, this whole thing was his fault. As for Sellie? Sellie made her nervous, but she knew things Soul Selector didn't, like Aphrodite's manna hoard. It might be wise to keep her around for a while. It pained her, but it looked like Death would get his way.

"Oh, all right," she conceded gracelessly.

"Yeah!" Death cheered. "We're a team. Jesse is safe!"

CHAPTER THIRTY

Jesse had had enough. She was surrounded by ancient old fools and twitching psychopaths. It was an unmanageable situation, and there was nobody she could trust. Soul Selector and Death were trying to help, but she had no faith in them. They were soft hitters. There was obviously a bigger, meaner, madder power at work, and that power meant to annihilate her for whatever reason. What the hell had she ever done to aggravate Aphrodite? What a total bitch!

Jesse teleported back to the pool. She didn't want to hang around waiting for Soulie and Death to come up with some last chance strategy. Their incompetency stretched her nerves, and her need to see Norrie was overpowering. She had been away from the pool too long already. It was her narcotic. The pool fed her; it kept her sanity intact, despite all the madness around her. It would take a few minutes before Soul Selector realized she was gone, but a few minutes was all she needed.

The pool responded to her immediately. Beneath its surface, shadows and sunlight swirled in a slow, lazy current until the dark and light melded and the Donegal beach where Norrie lived came into view. White-topped waves crashed against the shore, and rain clouds piled in from the Atlantic. The wind cracked the dune grass into a frenzied warning for the storm about to land.

A lone figure walked along the shoreline, and Jesse instinctively knew it was Norrie. Her footprints weaved in and out along the scalloped tidemark. Her crimson shawl streaked out behind her like a war banner. Norrie trudged head down into the wind, pausing once in a while to look out to sea and allow the wind to pummel her.

What was she thinking? She looked so sad. Jesse hung over the edge and let her hands and knees sink into the muddy bank. She leaned further over. *What if I fell in?*

She dipped her face to the water. Donegal was still there. She could smell the salt, and the wind flung stinging sand against her cheeks. She blinked. Surely it couldn't be this easy? Her heart beat harder, and she sunk her head further into the water. Her ears went under, and the wind howled and whipped at her hair. *Oh my God. I can do it. I can go there.*

With one last push, she went tumbling through. A world of sensation crashed around her. Chill, tumultuous air swallowed her up, while the scent of salty sea scoured her sinuses. She slammed flat on her back onto the beach. Sand and stones knocked the air from her lungs, and she sucked a glorious salty breath back in.

Why didn't I do this before? Why did I listen to that idiot and her stupid rules? Did Soul Selector even know you could step through into the real world? Her pool was a freakin' portal, and Jesse bet Soulie had no idea. No idea at all.

The surf roared. Sand shifted underneath her. She lay rejoicing at the chill and damp seeping through her shirt onto the skin of her back. She was freezing. Her flesh goose-bumped, but it felt delicious. All of this, the cold air, her wet back, the rumble of surf drowned by incoming thunder, all of it—did all this sensation mean she was alive? She was a visitor in a place where she did not belong. Was she a ghost?

Jesse struggled to her feet. Her balance was bad. She kept slipping and sliding on the slope of sand. By standing upright, all her impressions of this world changed. Jesse took a staggering step forward. The muscles in her legs burned. Her chest hurt. She was sucking in air as heavy as iron. Reentry was tough.

Up ahead, she saw Norrie coming steadily toward her. There was no indication she had seen Jesse as yet or that a woman had just materialized before her on the beach. Jesse waited as she approached, her gaze zigzagging over every feature of Norrie's face. She knew she was staring wildly, probably like a mad woman. Norrie kept coming closer. Her face was flushed. Tendrils of blond hair flew free from under her hat, her shawl billowed around her shoulders. She was swirling and windswept and totally organic within the gathering storm. Everything about her was movement and vibrant, thrumming life. Jesse took a step toward her and stopped. Norrie turned. Her back was to the water and she faced Jesse head on, and looked right through her.

She can't see me. I'm invisible. I'm a ghost, or as good as a ghost. The thought was crushing. Norrie passed by so close Jesse could smell her perfume. Her fingers itched to reach out and touch her sleeve, to try to detain her.

Why had she expected it to be easy? Nothing that had happened since her death had made sense or gone the way she wanted. And here she was, back on earth with her soul mate, so why should that be any less complicated?

Norrie walked past her, her head down, eyes empty. She stopped and again looked over to where Jesse stood. Jesse held her breath. Norrie's gaze slid over her to scan along the beach before returning to bore through her. She turned toward the surf and looked out at the lowering horizon and its bands of gathering clouds. Her shoulders slumped. With a deep sigh, Norrie walked on, paused, but only for an instant, before wheeling on her heel and heading straight for the sea. She loosened the shawl and let it fly free from her neck. Her coat slipped from her shoulders to lie heaped beside her abandoned shoes. Norrie walked on into the tide. She plowed through the waves until she was knee high, waist high, she was almost chest high when the waves finally knocked her over and she disappeared.

Jesse watched in horror, her gaze glued on the big gray breakers. Norrie didn't surface. Jesse focused on where she had last seen the blond head dipping under the waves. She took a huge gulp of air and plunged after her into the Atlantic.

CHAPTER THIRTY-ONE

I used to love this old pool." Sellie sighed.

Soul Selector scowled and inched closer to it.

"But you can't trust it." Sellie turned and examined the rest of the grotto. "I like what you've done here with the jacarandas. Looks good."

"Jesse did it," Death said.

"Hang on a minute," Soul Selector said. "What do you mean you can't trust it?"

Sellie shrugged. "You just can't."

"What's wrong with my pool?"

"Incoming." Death stuck a finger in his ear and signaled for quiet.

"I'm only referring to my own experience." Sellie's vagueness was annoying.

"What do you mean?" Soul Selector persisted. "Why can't you trust it?"

"Sh!" Death had both fingers in his ears now. "I'm getting a fax."

"I mean it plays tricks on you," Sellie said.

Soul Selector snorted. "Maybe on you. It's never tricked me."

"Quiet, you guys. I can't hear a thing," Death said.

"How do you know it hasn't?" Sellie asked.

"Because I'm not stupid."

"Ooh, whiplash." Sellie grabbed at the nape of her neck. "Quick, get me a chiropractor to undo the damage of your acerbic wit."

"Please. Would you mind keeping the noise down?" Death hissed and turned away, his fingers still plugging his ears.

"At least I've never sat in a hole for a million years."

"You couldn't find a hole unless you looked between your ears." Sellie hit back.

"If I did you'd probably sit in it."

"That does it! You two are so selfish." Death dematerialized in a huff.

"Is he always that dramatic?" Sellie asked.

"Every night is Emmy night."

Seconds later, Death popped back pale and sweating.

"That was quick," Soul Selector said.

"Is everything all right?" Sellie asked.

"No, it isn't." Death gasped for air. "I feel sick."

"You rematerialized too fast." Soul Selector felt obliged to point out.

"It's not that." Death was waving a finger toward the pool. "Jesse is in there."

"Huh?" Soul Selector looked to where he was pointing. It dawned on her that she hadn't seen Jesse since the audience with Zeus. The emergence of Sellie from the pit had taken up all her attention.

"She's in the pool," Death babbled. "I got a message from my office. Jesse's down as a double entry in the logbook."

"What?" Sellie and Soul Selector asked in unison.

"She's already dead. She can't go and die on me again. It's greedy, and she's weally screwed up my ops system. The girls in the office are furious."

"She's dying?" Soul Selector stood at the edge of the pool and glared at its surface. "In here?" The water was perfectly calm; there was barely a ripple. "What? Why?" She couldn't form her question. She wasn't even sure what her question was. What was Death burbling on about?

"What are you burbling about?" she finally said.

"Tricky things, scrying pools." Sellie came and stood beside her. "Oh, there she is. Who's that with her?"

"What?" Soul Selector could see nothing. What was the imbecile talking about?

"Whoever she is she's not on my schedule." Death had joined them at the pool. "Why is everyone trying to jump the queue today?" He was very miffed.

"I don't know, but let's go see," Sellie said.

"See what?" Soul Selector glared as hard as she could. Slowly, the silt and muddy shadows shifted. She wasn't sure, but thought she could make out the vague outline of a miserable, rain-soaked beach.

"It's raining," she said, pleased that she could finally see what the other two were prattling on about.

"It's more than raining," Sellie said. "It's a full on Atlantic gale. Jump!" She plunged in headfirst, soaking the other two with the splash.

"What the—" Soul Selector jumped back, shaking water drops from her cloak.

"Oh, now that's clever," Death said and leaped in after Sellie. Soul Selector stood shocked. What in Hades? He'd jumped in, and he was usually such a wimp. Cautiously, she toed the water. Nothing happened.

She pushed her foot further in. Still nothing happened. She took another teeny-weeny toe poke…and slipped.

"Aaah!" She landed with a thud on Donegal sand. Death and Sellie were standing nearby. Their hair whipped crazily in the wind, and Sellie's cloak streamed away from her like crazy bat wings.

"What kept you?" Death asked. "We're freezing." Somewhere along the way, he had acquired a bright yellow sailing jacket, waterproof pants, and a captain's sailing cap. He looked very snug and shipshape.

"So what happens next?" Soul Selector asked. She had no idea why they were here. She hated the earth realm. Everything was so textured and smelly. The wind was battering her senseless, and she envied Death his weatherproof garb.

"We need to get them out." Sellie pointed to two tiny heads bobbing up and down on the distant sea swell.

"In all Hades!" Soul Selector gasped. Her soul mates! And what was Jesse doing with Norrie? This was a blatant disregard of the rules. *Her* rules. "What do they think they're doing?"

"They're drowning," Death informed her.

"Oh no, you don't!" she yelled at him. "It's bad enough one of them is prematurely dead. I'm damned if you're dumping the other one on me."

"She's not on my schedule," Death shouted back. "Everyone's cheating."

"You cheat death by avoiding it, you idiot!"

"Your friends are failing to float," Sellie interrupted. "We really need to get them out. Can either of you swim?"

"He's in the waterproofs." Soul Selector placed a hand on Death's back and launched him into the tide. She'd been doing that a lot recently and enjoying it. "Go and save somebody for once."

A large wave ebbed away from the shore, dragging him out with it. His squeal could be heard over the howling gale.

Sellie moved closer.

"It's hard time here, isn't it?" she asked.

"So?"

"So can you make it soft? That way we can try to slow it down, or maybe even reverse it?"

Soul Selector didn't like the question. She was not very good at playing with hard versus soft time. Good at talking about it, but not actually manipulating it.

"I can't do that," she said. "Only the gods are allowed to change Earth time. It's the rules."

Sellie clucked her tongue disapprovingly. "What use have the rules ever been to you?"

Soul Selector bristled, Sellie was talking nonsense, as if a mere soul selector could twiddle time like the hands on a wristwatch.

"Rules are necessary things. The more they annoy the better they are," she said, a little snippily.

Something shifted. She barely noticed it at first until the waves began to rise and fall in slow motion and the wind fell against her face like a heavy, damp blanket. Death reappeared dripping wet at her side. His whole body shook and seawater poured out of the sleeves of his jacket. Sellie had illegally tampered with the time flow and managed to do so easily.

"I can see why you were retired early." Soul Selector sulked. "Flawed model," she muttered to Death.

"You pushed me in!" He shook with cold down to his boots.

"And now you're a hero," she said, looking behind him. "Where are they?"

"Jesse is back by the pool and the other one is over there." Sellie pointed to a solitary walker farther up the beach. "She's coming this way, only this time there'll be no Jesse to befuddle her."

"It's illegal for the likes of you to turn back time," Soul Selector said.

"It saved them," Sellie pointed out.

"If you could change the flow of time then why did I have to be pushed in?" Death wanted to know.

"Because it was fun," Soul Selector snapped.

"Because hard and soft time don't affect you here." Sellie ignored her and explained it to him. "You're an otherworld entity. The rules of this world aren't applicable to you. If I had failed to tweak time then at least you were there to help in your own special way. Think of yourself as Plan B."

"He'd have killed them both," Soul Selector said. "That's his own special way. Unless you're a dog," she added, "dogs go free."

Death refused to look at her. "Can we go home now?" he asked. He looked miserable. "This wealm's wules of cold and wet seem to be applicable to me."

"Really? You must be supersensitive," Sellie said with approval in her voice.

"Why, thank you." He brightened up a little. "I am a little sensitive."

"Oh, for heaven's sake, I'm calling a quorum on your mutual appreciation society. We need to get back to the pool before Jesse does something else beyond stupid." Soul Selector was anxious to catch up with Jesse and tie her to the nearest jacaranda tree until she had an idea of what to do with her.

"Okay then, back through the portal, I suppose." Sellie trudged off up the beach.

Portal? Soul Selector watched as Sellie retraced her steps and Death squelched dejectedly behind her. The wind leaped out of its engineered lethargy and slapped her sharply in the face. It was a wake-up call. Time had returned to normal, and Norrie was trudging down the beach, coming closer. Soul Selector had no idea how to transport back to the pool. Sellie's cloak billowed in the wind, enveloping both her and Death. The cloak snapped away into nothingness taking Sellie and Death with it.

"No." Soul Selector hurried after them. She was unsure how Sellie did it. She hurried after the footprints hoping there was a way she could hang on to their coattails. Her eyes blurred and the beach wavered. She lost balance as sand slid out from under her feet throwing her forward onto the muddy grass on the banks of her pool. Jacaranda blossom framed the branches above her head, and she had to hold on to a tree trunk to steady herself. Sellie, Jesse, and Death stood a few feet away. Death was dressed in another lurid shell suit. He was warm and dry and looking much happier. Soul Selector sort of regretted throwing him in the tide. Jesse stood to the side as sullen as any teenager forced to hang with the grownups. She seemed in a world of her own barely noticing the other two.

"What were you thinking?" Soul Selector descended on her at full volume.

"I'm not going to wait around for you and Typhoid Mary here to come up with a plan. I'm going to look after myself," Jesse roared back.

"Maway was a good friend of mine." Death looked hurt.

Sellie dropped an arm around Jesse's hunched shoulders and was allowed to keep it there, much to Soul Selector's disgust. Sellie sneaked in everywhere. She'd have to keep an eye on her.

"You can't go back to earth. You're dead. You're breaking all the rules!" Her worry made her shout louder.

"Give the kid a break," Sellie said. "It's hard for her. She shouldn't be here. It's normal for her to want to follow her heart."

"Like you're the expert?" Soul Selector said. "Where did your errant soul mate end up, huh?"

Sellie stiffened, then looked away. She didn't answer.

"I knew it!" Soul Selector said. "She's sitting in another hole somewhere."

"I don't care if she's sitting on your head," Jesse said. "I want to be with Norrie and soon, or else I'm going back."

"If you go back you'll kill her," Sellie said. "She walked into the sea, Jesse. What does that tell you?"

"Why did she do that?" Death asked. "My office was in turmoil. She was completely unscheduled. We can't have people dying on a whim. Hades will have my hide for wallpaper." He looked worried. Aphrodite was an A-list bitch, but the Lord of the Underworld was a complete bastard to work for. For an instant, Soul Selector felt sorry for him, then she remembered what he'd gotten her into.

"Good," she said. "He can turn your spangled hide into a disco ball for all I care."

"Why did Norrie want to kill herself?" Jesse asked Sellie.

"She's always been on the verge," Sellie said. "A singular soul mate is a sad, lonely being, an unnatural creation. Soul mates are destined to exist in a state of togetherness, and when left alone they drift into a terrible depression that dogs their existence. They live in a state of non-fulfillment no matter how materially successful they may be. For Norrie, despair is always waiting around the corner because you aren't."

"But I would have made all that better!" Jesse exploded. "Yet she didn't even see me."

"She couldn't see you because you don't exist in her reality. You died long ago, Jesse. And by being there, by being close to her, you magnified her despair to the point of suicide."

"I'm sorry, Jesse," Death said. "The dead can't go back."

"And especially not soul mates," Soul Selector added. "Especially."

"So I'll kill her if I'm with her?" Despair filled Jesse's eyes. "Well, that sucks."

"Yes. It does," Sellie said.

"Will she remember she tried to kill herself today? I couldn't bear for her to." Jesse roughly brushed the last of her tears away.

"But she didn't," Sellie said. "Time changed. She didn't meet you, she didn't react, so she didn't harm herself."

"But if Norrie did die would we be together?" Jesse asked.

"No. She'll be put in the reincarnation queue and that will be that." Soul Selector was tired of pointing out the obvious to a kid who wouldn't listen. "Due to your philanthropy for the canine species you are now seriously out of sync with each other. It will be thousands of years until you line up again, that's if Aphrodite hasn't exterminated you first. Imagine star-crossed lovers, only one of you is an asteroid heading for a black hole." The silence that greeted her outburst made Soul Selector wonder if she'd been too blunt. But what the heck, the kid had asked. Why not tell her the truth?

Chapter Thirty-two

I'm sorry." Norrie held Loa's gaze. It was unbearable to see the hurt in her beautiful eyes. She had had this conversation countless times with many other lovers. The "The End" conversation. The "It's Over" one. This time it hurt her more. It was frightening, but she had to do it, for both their sakes.

"Wow," Loa said, her voice thickening. She took an audible swallow and looked away. "I thought we were doing well. Didn't see this coming." She looked confused and embarrassed and tried to compose herself by picking lint from her skirt. "Can I ask why? I mean did I do anything?" It was an honest, straightforward question, nothing plaintive or wheedling about it.

"No," Norrie said. "It definitely isn't you." She was wary of the old platitudes she used to trot out so easily. "And it's not me either," she said quickly. "I'm not blaming either of us. No one's at fault. In my heart, I know you're not what I need. You're lovely. You're a gorgeous, kind, caring person, and you should know that about yourself."

Loa was crying now. Tears freely ran down her face. Norrie drew her into her arms.

"I'm not like you," she said. "I'm not magical. I can't reach out and help people. I hide in my songs and play act through them. One day, I'll be what I write about."

"You're hollow. You feel hollow," Loa said. "I know what this is. I feel like that, too, sometimes. This is the closest I have ever been to where I emotionally want to be. And to be honest, I'm afraid to be on my own."

"I get frightened, too." Norrie understood what Loa was saying. "I get bad dreams and days when I don't want to be on the planet, never mind out of bed." She took a deep breath and said, "I suffer from chronic depression, Loa. And I'm slipping into a bad place and I want to be there alone. I can't have you around me at the moment. I need to focus on myself. It sounds selfish, but that's the way it is."

She had been fine, actually. She'd even been applauding her new relationship. Loa stabilized her. They had so much in common, especially on an emotional level. If humans gave out a humming noise then she and Loa were on the same wavelength; they buzzed along on the same megahertz. She had felt great. There was a fabulous passion between them, a fantastic heat. And then black clouds began to gather. Literally. She had been on the beach watching a storm off to the west of Arranmore. Storms usually energized her, she loved them, but this one was a big, black bastard. It had crowded in on her giving her migraines and tossing her emotions about as if she was in its epicenter, and it sucked the soul right out of her.

She'd returned home windswept and miserable, and it had only gotten worse. In the following days, she slipped back in the depression she knew so well. The descent into this pit was well mapped out across her life. She knew it for what it was and what she had to do to emerge from it. Loa was simply a casualty. Yet another one, like her performance career, and every previous lover. All sacrificed to the monstrous parasite that sucked on her mind, body, and soul.

"I'm sorry, Loa." She was crying now.

"I understand." Already Loa was gathering her coat and purse. "Really I do. If it's not the perfect fit, you don't want it. I can be like that, too. But for me you were a real close fit, Norrie. I want you to know that."

Norrie watched Loa drive away, torn as to whether she'd done the right thing even though she knew it would be cruel to use her as a life raft. In this life, Norrie had to learn over and over how to keep herself afloat.

CHAPTER THIRTY-THREE

Jesse had her back to the pool. She sat several yards away in a copse of willow, all of her own making. The green curtain gave her privacy. She felt exposed and angry. Her impatience had put Norrie into danger. She was so powerless. No matter what she did, they might never be united. Her life, or death, or whatever it was, was a litany of error, bad luck, and downright shittiness. She had to be with Norrie, absolutely had to, but how?

"You've made another lovely environment." Sellie's voice came from somewhere behind her. "Were you a landscape architect before you died?"

"I was a teenager."

"Ah." For some reason Sellie took that as an invitation to sit beside her. "I thought you looked young, but it's hard to tell on the Fields. It could have been your essence made you seem younger."

Jesse grunted. She pushed up onto her heels preparing to walk away.

"Have you any new ideas on how to get to her?"

The question held her in place. "I wish I had. Do you?"

"No." Sellie looked around her, very taken with the greenery. "You've been very ingenious the way you've managed this place," she said. "Most souls would have eaten the orange and that would be that."

"So I'd be fast asleep when Aphrodite came for me?" With a snort, Jesse sat back down.

"Or she might not have noticed you at all."

Jesse thought this over then said, "She would have. She has a trigger, and it's not me."

"Trigger?"

"She wants something. It's not me, but I'm somehow involved. I'm not her real target otherwise you'd be talking to a piece of toast."

Sellie went quiet. Jesse knew she'd hit home. "Those other guys..." She nodded toward Soul Selector and Death. "They think she wants to finish me off, but they're wrong."

Sellie looked pensive. Jesse could sense there was an internal struggle going on, so she pressed further.

"What is the deal with her?" she asked. She might as well try to get all the information she could out of Sellie. The soul selector looked far too comfortable on her little tuft of grass to be on the move anytime soon. She'd joined Jesse for a reason; she wanted to talk.

"She's like all the gods. She's a complete control freak," Sellie said. The answer was a cop-out and Jesse was disappointed. She'd thought Sellie would open up and tell her what was really going on. Then Sellie cleared her throat and continued. "The big thing up here is manna, or god fuel if you like. And one of the best ways to harvest it is through soul mate love. It's the easiest way." Sellie settled into her story, and Jesse realized she was getting more than she'd bargained for. Sellie was a storyteller, and proverb preacher, a self-taught raconteur, and Jesse had opened a million-year floodgate.

"When the gods realized mankind was more than animal," Sellie began her story, "and that they had souls and that these souls generated energy, they set about trying to harness it. The energy was manna, a divine food, and love gave out the biggest amount, closely followed by the deepest evil. Love and hate are polar emotions that release the same energy though they flavor it in different ways. The end result is always fodder for the gods, and they don't care if the source is good or evil."

Now this was interesting. Jesse listened, not moving a muscle for fear of breaking Sellie's flow. "Of course there was huge in-family wrangling about which flavor was the best and who generated the most, the lovers or the haters. Obviously, Aphrodite wanted love to be the best. She was the goddess of love so that would give her the monopoly. Atë, her half sister and the goddess of ruin, wanted hate to be the main propagator. So they had a war. Humanity was split in two, the armies for good and the legions of evil, even though that was not the true representation of either goddess. Ares complained, only he should start wars among humanity, so he petitioned Zeus to step in. And he did. Zeus decreed that out of the millions of human souls, a few soul mates be created and only they could produce manna through their love."

"So Aphrodite won."

"No. Zeus is wily. He has a large, psychotic family to keep in check so he knows all the tricks. He created the notion of soul mates, preordained souls that connect time after time across infinity to meet, fall in love, and make manna. But he did not decree that the souls be from Aphrodite's army."

"The souls could be evil?" This shocked Jesse. Was she evil? Was that why she died too soon and lost her soul mate? Was she being punished?

"That was the compromise," Sellie said. "Soul mates were a new concept, and they could belong to either goddess. Even bad people fall in love. All that concerned Zeus and the other gods was that manna was made, and as I said before, they don't care what flavor."

"Am I evil? Is that why Aphrodite wants to destroy me?"

"Do you feel evil? Have you done evil things?"

Jesse blinked stupidly. "I don't know. I don't think I had time to."

"Jesse, you're not being punished here. You genuinely got caught up in one of Death's trawls. He feels awful about it," Sellie said. "Aphrodite told Zeus she wanted to clean up her department. What she proposes for you is harsh, but Soulie and Death are doing their best to prevent it. They'll come up with a plan, you'll see."

Jesse's eyes moistened. "I don't want to be dead," she said. "I want to live. I want to be with Norrie. That's all. There's nothing else in the world I want but that."

Sellie nodded sympathetically. "It's how you're made, Jesse. And believe me, Norrie feels exactly the same, except she has no idea you ever existed."

"I can't bear to feel like this for eternity. Maybe it's best to let Aphrodite destroy me." She struggled against her tears.

"I don't think Aphrodite will do that, and I think you suspect that, too."

"What will happen to Norrie?" She was foremost on Jesse's mind. Norrie was the real victim here.

"She'll grow old never finding the love she is looking for. Then she will die and eventually be reincarnated only to go through it all again, unless of course we can get you two resynchronized."

"Can we?" Jesse asked. She sounded pathetic, even to her own ears.

"We can try. I think we've been too easygoing, too form-filling." Her gaze drifted over to where Soul Selector trampled up and down waving her arms in the air, raving about something or other while a doleful Death sat nearby picking at grass stems.

"I can see phase two is going well," she muttered.

As they watched, Death froze, jammed a finger in his ear, and held up a hand to Soul Selector to shut up.

"Not another fax," Jesse said. "Who's fallen off a cliff now?" Then Death was waving them over. He was practically dancing with excitement. Soul Selector was scowling when Sellie and Jesse joined them.

"Disco squirrel has some news," she said. Sellie and Jesse waited.

"The office called," Death said. "JC Waites is taxiing for takeoff. She's got an ETA for tomorrow."

"And work is so slow you have to dance?" Jesse was unimpressed.

"Who is JC Waites?" Soul Selector asked.

"The woman in the coma," Death said, his excitement deflating rapidly, "at the hospital." He looked hurt.

"What hospital? Who?" Soul Selector was getting annoyed.

"Loa knows her," Jesse explained. "Her charity is looking for organ donors and JC Waites is on the waiting list."

"And who's Loa?" Sellie asked.

"Norrie's fwiend," Death said. "Don't you see?" Nobody seemed to see, so he sighed heavily, and began to elaborate. "Jesse can use her body for a while." He beamed a wide, proud smile and awaited the accolades.

"But," Sellie frowned, "she's in a coma. She's dying, so how can you put Jesse in a spent body? Do you expect it to heal?"

Death swung his gaze from Sellie to Soul Selector and back again, expecting some sort of reaction that he wasn't getting. "Well," he said, "That's the soul selecting side, isn't it? The quest was to help hide Jesse. This way we can get her away from Aphwodite and back into the living world. She can stay until JC's body gives out."

"I'm to die all over again? That's your famous plan?" Jesse said.

"It is a good hiding place," Sellie said. She looked at Jesse thoughtfully.

"He's doing it again." Soul Selector pointed at Death. "He's meddling and it will turn out the worse for me."

"Look on the bright side, for the short time that she's there, we can hook her up with her soul mate," Sellie said. "And when she dies, they'll be better synchronized."

Death nodded. "That was my plan. Only I hadn't thought it out."

"That's good. Well done, you," Sellie told him. He preened.

"Jesse will be in a coma. We don't even know if soul mates can operate with one of them in an altered state," Soul Selector said. She was in a sour mood because the plan was outside her control.

"Norrie visits JC all the time," Death said. "She cares for her enough as it is."

"We just need them to be in the same room even for a minute for the soul mate magic to kick in." Sellie was so up for the plan it pushed Soul Selector in the opposite direction for no other reason than to be contrary.

"I'll do it."

Nor did Soul Selector feel particularly confident about her soul mate magic. It had not always been on target. "It won't work," she said. "This JC sounds too far gone. She's not even conscious. There's not enough time."

"I'll do it."

"How much time is not enough time?" Sellie said. "I mean, she's a soul mate. She meets the love of her life and their love lasts forever. Their bodies won't, but their love will. The love only has to spark, just once, and they're away!"

"For the third and final time, I'll do it!" Jesse's exasperation exploded among them like shrapnel.

"I'll do it." She calmed down quickly once she had their attention. "I'll do anything to be with her. I'll do it."

Chapter Thirty-four

The waspish buzz in her ear brought Soul Selector to Aphrodite's temple in double quick time. She materialized before the throne, twitching with nerves. She had been expecting a debriefing from the goddess after their impromptu audience with Zeus. It had been hanging over her like an atomic mushroom cloud. The floor was barely solid under her feet before Aphrodite's anger unfurled.

"You backstabbing bitch!"

"My lady," she said, and tried to bow elegantly, but it turned into an awkward, angular jerk. "I was only there to collect my ward. Zeus found her on the Fields—"

"Shut up! Did I say you could talk?"

Under her feet, she could feel the rumble of volcanoes. Soul Selector's mouth grew dry and tasted of ash. She was sure there'd been an eruption on earth. The anger streaming from the goddess burned the air. It slithered through the temple like lava, thick and slow moving, and thoroughly vicious. Her cool, unflappable handmaidens began to look overheated and uncomfortable.

"You set me up. You welshed on me to my father. How could you let that stupid old buzzard get involved in this department's business? In my business!"

It was frustrating to be told to shut up then asked a stream of questions she ached to answer. Soul Selector kept her lips firmly sealed despite the fact it was Death who had "welshed" on the goddess and her slushy plan, not her, and now she was getting it in the neck. She'd be avenged on the grubby little gravedigger if it took a thousand years.

"Where is the little cow?"

This brought Soul Selector out of her reverie of the many ways to punish Death. *Cow? There's a cow?* She risked a response.

"Cow, my lady? Is there to be a sacrifice?"

"No, you dolt! The girl, where's the freakin' girl?" Aphrodite's screech made everyone in the temple recoil. A swan honked back in answer while everyone else, clerks, servants, general devotees, shrank back trying to make themselves as small a target as possible. The handmaidens shot Soul Selector hate-filled looks. They would be the ones dealing with Aphrodite's anger later, not her.

"The soul mate, idiot," Aphrodite continued to scream. "Why in Hades do I bother with you." It wasn't really a question, and Soul Selector stiffened. This was the worst audience she'd ever had with Aphrodite, and she carried bruises inside and out from previous meetings.

"She's…um, she's at the scrying pool." She was shocked to find she genuinely didn't want to tell Aphrodite. This was borderline insurrection. "We're preparing a place for her."

"Oh? Where's that then?"

"A vacant body on the mortal plane. We'll have just enough time for the soul mates to be realigned before the host body ceases to function." It was a good plan. It was downright clever, even if it wasn't her own. "Then we can reincarnate them together later and collect a manna harvest." This had to put her back in Aphrodite's good graces.

"Go get her."

"Pardon?"

"Go get her."

"But she's all ready to jump into the host." Soul Selector was confused. The plan was a win-win. Didn't Aphrodite get it?

"Get her!"

"But, Zeus—" She stopped mid sentence. Aphrodite actually hissed. She hissed like a reptile. Soul Selector shut up immediately. Her heart hammered. She was afraid. Afraid for herself, afraid for Jesse. Aphrodite had other plans. Bad plans. Plans she wasn't sharing with her soul selector.

"Now get out." Aphrodite's temper was no longer red hot. It was turning chilly. A freezing mist began to shroud her throne. She shone from within its milky depths like an ice-cold diamond. Around her dais, her handmaidens began to ice over. Their skin, hair, even their eyelashes sugared up like frosted cake ornaments. Soul Selector prepared to dematerialize as fast as she could, but Aphrodite raised a hand and she found herself stuck to the marble floor. A numbing cold crept up her shins and cramped her leg muscles.

"Take the trade door," the goddess said.

It was incredibly abusive. Soul Selector felt acute shame. Her abilities and usefulness were being openly questioned. She was humiliated. She had somehow failed Aphrodite. Head bowed, she walked toward the trade door at the rear of the great hall. As she passed, temple business recommenced as staff and patrons alike pretended not to notice her quiet exit.

When she drew level with the throne, she couldn't help a sad, sideways peek at Aphrodite's profile. It was magnificent. The most beautiful thing imaginable. As elegant as cut glass, as pale as cream, and as hard as flint. A splintering noise came from the dais. Two handmaidens, now no more than icy lumps, toppled down the throne steps. The nymphs had frozen to death at Aphrodite's feet. She didn't even notice. Her mood was lightening now. The icy mist dissipated. Melt water ran from her throne steps and trickled to where her handmaidens sat. Ice water began to drip from them. It seeped from their thawing hair and bodies, and from the hems of their togas. It trickled down their stiff, aching faces. Soul Selector saw the melt water on their cheeks mix with tears as the nymphs slowly defrosted from their icy agony.

She turned her face away from the harrowing scene and noticed the door. Or rather she noticed the guards standing impassively beside it. A small wooden doorway sat tucked behind the golden finery of Aphrodite's throne. It was noticeable because of its simple plainness in the midst of the temple's ostentation. And because of the huge, bare-chested, turbaned guards that stood, cross-armed, on either side of it. They were like twin genies out of the same lamp. Wicked looking scimitars hung at their sides.

This had to be the manna store Sellie had been talking about. Soul Selector would have given anything to see inside it. What did it mean? Why was Aphrodite amassing stocks of divine energy? There was only one explanation that Soul Selector could think of. Aphrodite meant to dispose of the old buzzard. The very thought shook Soul Selector to her bones, so hard she was sure bystanders could hear her rattle. Then the trade door was before her, and it was a relief to be leaving the temple totally ignored.

Chapter Thirty-five

A re you sure about this?"
Sellie and Jesse walked under swaying boughs of lilac-blue jacaranda blossoms that never faded.

"Yes," Jesse said. "What else is there? I may be lying like a log on a hospital bed, but at least Norrie and I will be in the same timeline and hopefully reincarnated together later."

"True."

"Will you be in charge of this little escapade?" Jesse asked.

"Well…it's not my watch, is it?" She patted Jesse on the shoulder. "Soulie will look after you just fine. I know you feel she dropped the ball, but believe me, she's struggling with an unusual set of circumstances, and none of it of her own making."

Jesse did not look convinced, but the re-materialization of Soul Selector into the grove closed the conversation.

"Well? What did our wonderful goddess want?" Sellie asked.

"Jesse. Again. So much for the seven days Zeus gave us."

Sellie frowned at this. "That's a bit naughty."

"And I think I saw the manna store," Soul Selector blurted. "The door behind her throne with two big hooligan guards."

"Told you so."

"Do you think she's planning a coup?" Soul Selector felt silly saying it.

Sellie shrugged. "Why not? That lot are always having domestics. They need a social services plan."

"It's a go!" Death popped up out of nowhere. He was wearing baby blue fatigues and looked as locked and loaded as the color would allow. "JC is in her last few hours. We need to move, people!"

"Do we have a plan?" Jesse was nervous. "And by plan I mean a scheme or method of procedure for the advancement of an agreed object or goal, not some 'by the seat of your blueberry pants' heist."

Death looked hurt. "I do have a plan," he said. "And a scheme. And this is periwinkle, not blueberry." He caressed his hip. "I've been to war. It's exhausting."

"Look, kid," Soul Selector said to Jesse. "All you have to do is lie down and die. It's not like you haven't rehearsed."

"What happens now?" Sellie asked. Soul Selector's face hardened. She resented the question. This was none of Sellie's business, and it was time she drew the line.

"Captain Coffin here will go do his mojo, and I'll follow with Jesse."

"It's all about timing," Death said. "One soul slips out as the other enters. Jesse can last several hours in a coma, giving Soul Selector time to get Norrie to the hospital. It would be nice if they could meet up before Jesse cwoaks."

"You're such an old romantic," Jesse said. He gave her a delighted smile and she scowled back.

"What do you want me to do?" Sellie asked.

"Nothing. It's all under control. Go and have a cup of tea or something. Find a nice hole to sit in." Soul Selector turned back to Death. "Let's go, Necro Boy." They had to get Jesse out of the Fields before Aphrodite came looking for her.

"I'm going down first to prep JC," he said. "Zeus will want a report so we'll have to keep within the wools."

Soul Selector sighed but agreed. "Be quick as you can. Send a fax when you're ready for us." Death was already an opaque outline as he evaporated away.

"How long will it take?" Jesse asked. Soul Selector shrugged.

"He can't rush it," Sellie spoke up. "It has to be a natural release. He wants to stick by the rules."

"He might as well. The gods sure as hell won't," Jesse muttered.

Soul Selector moved away silently seething. Why couldn't Sellie go find something else to do instead of hanging around her pool? She'd had her chance and she'd mucked it up. It made her nervous that a loser like Sellie was attaching herself to Jesse. Soul Selector did not want her lurking around like a ghoul waiting for something to go wrong. A horrible thought crawled into her mind. She was already in trouble with Aphrodite. What if Sellie was waiting for her to fall on her face so she could take over her old job again?

A gentle mental nudge broke up her thoughts. The whisper of periwinkle polyester slid through her synapses making her shudder. A "cooee" noise scratched away behind her eyes until they were dry and itchy. Death was such an irritant.

This was his come-hither. She looked across to Jesse. The kid stood alone on the other side of the pool. She looked tense, and rightly so. Soul Selector was aware Jesse was disappointed in her. She had not been a good guardian, but with this last little piece of unpleasantness, she would be able to make it up to her tenfold. She would mollycoddle her and Norrie's souls through a thousand lifetimes making sure they were happy and pumping out enough manna to feed the heavens for infinity.

Manna. Her thoughts spun back to Aphrodite and whatever the goddess had planned. That made her nervous and she didn't need it, especially with the task ahead.

"Jesse," she called and nodded at the slick surface of the pool. The waters were gray and greasy and not at all inviting.

It was as if they were warning her, but she hadn't the time or skill to work out why. She saw Sellie gazing at the surface with troubled eyes. She also had noticed the warning in the water. Soul Selector ignored her and approached the pool with Jesse but from separate sides. They stood facing each other, eyes locked. Soul Selector nodded once more. They jumped.

❖

Norrie was lucky. The elevator doors opened just as she approached, letting visitors out onto the ground floor. She stepped into the empty carriage and hit the button for ICU.

Charge nurse Rose Connelly was at the nursing station with two other staff. They were chewing toffees and wading through a tower of paperwork.

"Good evening," Norrie greeted Rose.

"Happy Valentine's to you." Rose looked up, happy for a distraction. "Why aren't you out on a hot date with some big Hollywood bucko?"

Norrie waved the envelope in her hand. "Because I'm delivering my Valentine cards first. Then I'm having a sexy evening in with champagne, a bubble bath, and me."

"There's no hope for the rest of us if you can't get a date on Valentine's Day." Rose tsked. "Is that for JC?" She nodded at the envelope.

Norrie nodded. "The chocolates are for you." She placed a heart shaped box on the desk.

"Ooh. Posh." Rose was appreciative. "Look, girls." She showed the box to her colleagues. "The diet is postponed for another week."

"And this"—Norrie produced a CD case from her coat pocket—"is for JC. The promised copy of the finished song. Loa said it was okay to bring it in."

"Have you seen Loa lately?" Rose asked.

"No, not for a while." She felt guilt ooze out of her. She had not been in contact with Loa since they'd broken up. Loa had wanted it that way, at least for now, though Norrie hoped there'd be something salvageable in time. "Why?"

Rose shrugged. "She seems sort of down." Norrie's guilt ratcheted up a notch. She pointed at the side ward.

"Is it okay to leave this by the bed?"

The phone rang and Rose shooed her away with one hand while reaching for the phone with the other. Norrie went over to JC's room and gently pushed the door open. The overhead lights were off with only the bedhead lamp creating a dim halo around JC. Shadows pressed in from the corners. The beep and burp of machinery was the only sound. The room felt pensive and sad, and Norrie wondered how much of it was a projection of her own emotional state.

"Hi, JC." Rose had told her it was only proper to behave as normally as possible around a comatose person. Heaven knew what the subconscious could pick up. Norrie waggled the CD case. "I brought the new song as promised, though I'll leave it for Rose to play for you tomorrow morning." She set the CD beside the portable player and moved over to the bed. Now she was in the meager circle of light with JC. It felt spooky, as if the rest of the room was filled with ghosts and secrets. *I'm maudlin tonight. I don't want to be alone.*

"Today is Valentine's Day so I got you this. I'm sure it's not the first; you're a good-looking gal." She ripped open the envelope and set her card on the bedside table. "It's a wee bit twee, but the rest were too risqué, even for Rose's eyes." She sighed. "Romance is not what it used to be."

The card showed a fat cupid perched on a fluffy cloud. He was firing arrows at a red glitter heart, exploding it like a balloon. Norrie examined it again, just as she had at the shop. It was garish and not to her taste, but she'd felt compelled to buy it anyway.

"Aren't you the truth and a half?" she told the tattered heart. "Love hurts. Give me an aortal blood clot any day." Was it the light or did the arrows flare and almost shimmer as if in flight? Norrie blinked and the effect was lost. She set the card down and left the darkened room with a soft good night to JC.

Rose was still on the phone so Norrie headed for the elevator. She hadn't lied to Rose, though she wished she wasn't telling the truth. A bottle of Champagne waited in her car, and although she was genuinely looking forward to a long, luxurious bath, she would have liked a lover to share it with. But not a Hollywood bucko. The temptation to call Loa tonight was strong. Norrie shook the thought from her head. Loa was not booty call material; that had been apparent on their breaking up, and she—

A riot of activity burst out behind her.

Norrie turned to see Rose and several other staff racing toward JC's side ward. Unsure what was happening but growing more alarmed by the second, she retraced her steps. In the little side ward, JC's machinery was screaming. Lights flashed and the nurses were stripping back her bed linen.

"Move!"

Norrie stepped aside as a crash trolley thundered past her.

"You need to go now." Rose came and took her by the elbow and escorted her away. Over her shoulder, Norrie could see the choreography of emergency resuscitation played out.

"Okay. Okay. Sorry." She moved away and let Rose get back to work. Norrie stood shaking with shock. And because Loa had been on her mind only minutes ago, and because she knew Loa cared so much for JC, and because she had wanted her there anyway, Norrie scrabbled for her cell phone and dialed Loa's number.

Chapter Thirty-six

Soul Selector had no idea what to do next. The hospital was a bright, shiny box on the outskirts of Dungloe, and she hated it. Everywhere she looked humans were scuttling about, their psychic and spiritual frequencies completely congested with overwrought emotions. Humans gave her the heebie-jeebies.

Jesse stood quiet and withdrawn beside her. They were being drawn toward the hospital entrance. Death was directing them to JC's location.

"She's with me now." His voice echoed in her head. She could see Jesse was receiving the same communication. "We're on the top floor."

They drifted up stairwells unobserved by the few people who used these rather than the elevators. As they passed, people shivered or frowned or simply had a bad thought and carried on oblivious to the presence on the stairs with them. ICU was easy to find. Death called them to a side ward at the end of a long corridor, just past the empty nurses' station.

They reached the room where Death, dressed in hospital scrubs, hovered in a far corner. A more robust version of JC Waites than that lying on the bed stood beside him. They were watching a medical team try to defibrillate her earthly body. Death waved them over with a delighted welcome.

"Hi. This is JC," he said. She gave a nervous smile. "She's been a twooper." He patted her on the shoulder. "Most souls can't wait to get outta here, but JC was okay to hang on for you guys."

He became all business, abandoning JC temporarily with an apology to turn his attention to Jesse and part two of the plan. "I have to get your soul into JC's body before the heart restarts."

Soul Selector stepped back. She was redundant at this stage. It was strange to think that once Jesse's soul was ensconced in a human body all would go back to normal and her soul selecting work would go on as before. Zeus would be pleased she had resolved a problem within the allotted timeframe, and with minimum input required from him. There was also the hope that Aphrodite would lay off her because a manna harvest had been saved. Relief buzzed through her like a narcotic. She retreated further until she was lurking in the doorway, dispassionately watching the activity within. All Soul Selector needed was a few hours. Just long enough for Norrie to come to the hospital and reconnect with Jesse. Then they'd be more or less synchronized, and hallelujah to that.

From the corner of her eye she could see a woman sitting in a corner of the waiting area. A dark cloud of sorrow hovered over her head. It swirled around her like a black, relentless mass of insects, rising and falling on her with maddening inconsistency. Her body was hunched over and turned toward the elevators. She had to be waiting for someone. Soul Selector kept darting little glances her way, torn between the woman and the soul transfer going on in the side ward. Jesse had faded away to absolute nothingness in this realm. She was practically vapor. Death was drawing her spiritual essence toward the empty vessel lying on the bed. He had seconds left to make the swap complete.

Soul Selector locked in on the woman in the waiting room, trying to read her on a metaphysical level. She had to filter out a ton of the emotional garbage floating around in this world. There was a flood of it pouring in from every angle, and she was stuck in the middle of it without the filters of the pool to help. Her senses were unfocused and sluggish. And then she saw it, the faint glimmer of the woman's soul. There was something that set her apart from all the other souls in the building and let Soul Selector know beyond all doubt that this soul was one of hers; she was a soul mate.

Norrie! The woman was Norrie. How had she managed to appear at the hospital so soon? Soul Selector had not attempted to summon her yet. This was too strange. She strode down the corridor to the waiting area. She had no idea why Norrie was here, but the timing was excellent. Eerily excellent. She would commandeer Norrie's soul and make it move bodily toward JC's room. Jesse would be in her body in a matter of minutes. They would meet over the sickbed and her work would finally be done. The taste of success was honey on her tongue. They had done it. The plan had worked.

The elevator doors opened and Loa Ebele hurried onto the floor. Soul Selector froze. The impact of this woman's presence on her in the physical world was staggering. Peeking at her from the scrying pool was no comparison to being in the same physical dimension. Soul Selector reeled at the intensity of it.

Norrie and Loa embraced. Talking rapidly, Norrie led them down the corridor to the nurses' station, and straight toward Soul Selector.

"Soulie! Come away." The urgent call came from behind her. Sellie had materialized by JC's doorway and was calling to her. "Don't look at her. Get away!" But Soul Selector was rooted to the spot. The women advanced. They were charging down upon her like Custer's cavalry, and still she could not move. Norrie brushed past her but Loa, Loa walked right into her, right through her. Then Sellie was by her side tugging at her sleeve and Loa was staggering, sagging at her knees and Norrie was reaching out to catch her and the human world was spinning and Soul Selector felt…wrong. She felt so wrong, as if she had swallowed a cocktail of plutonium. She felt bitter and poisoned and doomed all in the same instant.

Sellie dragged her away. "No!" she was shouting. "No." She looked horrified and clung on to Soul Selector as hard as Soul Selector was clinging to her. They were both buckling under some unfathomable dread. Sellie gave her arm one more tug. A hard one, as if she had dredged up the last remnants of her strength and pulled Soul Selector along with her. They broke the surface of the pool and landed on its banks like thrashing fish. They were safely back in the Elysian Fields. Soul Selector was still in a state of collapse. She flailed about until Sellie's firm hand on her shoulder stilled her.

"What the hell was that?" she panted. She blinked away her tears, but more came. She had never cried in all her existence; she hadn't known she could cry, and now her tears were uncontrollable. "What happened? Where did you come from?"

"I was here." Sellie sounded exhausted. "Watching in the pool. And I saw him. I saw Eros. He was spying from a Valentine's card, and I realized Aphrodite knew about your plan and that she would spoil it."

Soul Selector rubbed at her damp eyes while she thought it through. She had already informed Aphrodite, in the loosest terms, about their plan for Jesse. "I told her before," she said.

"Oh." Sellie was surprised. "You trust her that much?"

"She's my goddess. Why shouldn't I? Anyway, Jesse is gone now. It's over."

"You shouldn't trust her." Sellie was blunt. "She wanted Jesse's soul and she always gets what she wants," she said. "She had Eros spy on you. She had Norrie show up unexpectedly and Loa, too. She pulled out all the stops. She wants to destroy you, Soulie."

"Why? I'm her Soul Selector. Why would she do that?" Soul Selector felt sick. All the worries she had tried to bury resurfaced.

The doubts she carried about Aphrodite being through with her flooded back. Had the goddess double-crossed her?

"What does she want with Jesse?" she said. Sellie's face closed over. "Why is she so determined to destroy her?" She persisted, certain that Sellie knew more than she was letting on.

"I don't know," Sellie said.

"She's gone to a lot of trouble sending Eros to spy on us. I don't understand why."

Sellie shrugged and rose from the bank to walk away.

"What happened with Loa?" Soul Selector asked. She was embarrassed that she had to ask, but she truly didn't know. She didn't know why she was so fascinated with the woman, or what had happened to her when Loa had walked onto the ICU floor, never mind right through her. It had been like living and dying all in the same instant. A sliver of intimacy and the laceration of grief and separation had almost ripped her apart.

"I have no idea." Sellie said, and walked on.

Chapter Thirty-seven

W hat are you trying to do to me?" Death's screech materialized before he did. Soul Selector and Sellie turned to meet him as he solidified by the scrying pool. "You left me down there with thwee of them! Thwee! Is this some kind of joke?"

"What are you talking about?" Soul Selector said. She was still shaken from her own experience and did not need his histrionics.

"Soul mates," he said. "You left me swamped with soul mates and no clue what to do with them. Soul mates are your department, and you just up and disappeared and left me with them."

"What?" She could see that he was angry to the point of tears, but she still had no idea what was wrong. "What are you going on about? Norrie was there to meet Jesse like we'd agreed." She didn't have to let him know that was probably Aphrodite's meddling rather than her own. "You did get Jesse into JC's body, didn't you?" A chill came into her stomach; that was the only thing she could think of that could have gone majorly wrong. Why would Aphrodite help her when she was more inclined to thwart? The heady scent of the goddess was everywhere in this.

"Yes! No!" He flung his arms in the air. "Loa distracted me. She distracted everyone! And I hesitated for just one second, and JC's heart kicked in and she survived. Against orders, I might add. Jesse is still with us." His eyes brimmed over. "My wecords are a mess because of you."

"Where's Jesse now?" Sellie asked. She exchanged a worried look with Soul Selector.

"Isn't she here?" He looked around. "I thought she would be. She left before me."

"Who's the third one?" Soul Selector asked.

"The third what?"

"Soul mate." Her patience was wearing thin. "You said there were three."

"Loa," he answered. "Loa's a soul mate. Didn't you know that?" He was genuinely perplexed and looked across to Sellie for verification. Soul Selector followed his gaze and exploded into a white-hot fury.

"You knew!" She advanced on Sellie. "How could you know? How can *he* know and I didn't see it? What is going on here? Tell me, or I swear I'll bury you up to your neck in that friggin' hole you like so much."

Sellie stared at her, her dark eyes huge with worry and guilt. "She's yours," she said.

"My what? I'd never seen her before last week."

"She's yours," Sellie repeated. "She's your soul mate."

"I've just said I've never—"

"She's yours, Soulie. Loa is, was, your soul mate." Sellie was staring at her, speaking calmly. "When you came here you forgot about her."

Soul Selector went quiet. She stared into the earnest depths of Sellie's eyes trying to assimilate what she had just said. Death watched them, agog, his mouth hanging open.

"How did that happen?" she said. She knew. She was sure she knew…but she wanted Sellie to say it, to confirm it.

"You died." It was hard for her to talk about it. Soul Selector could see that. "I was your Selector and you were one of my souls and I lost you." Her explanation was quiet and simple.

"Loa?" Soul Selector's voice was thick. It stuck in her throat. "She was yours too?"

"Yes. She was your soul mate. There was no one else for her but you."

And the truth of Loa's existence over the thousands of years lay open for them all to see. Born over and over with an aching, empty heart. Always alone, always missing an indefinable something. A half never made whole.

"I can't remember," Soul Selector whispered. "I can't remember a thing."

"You weren't meant to. It happened a long time ago," Sellie said. "You were always an impetuous, headstrong child. All seemed well, and then...I blame the pool. It told me nothing. It didn't warn me. One minute you were there and then you were gone."

"Gone?"

"You killed yourself." Sellie was blunt.

"Suicide? I committed suicide?" She turned to Death who took a step back under the intensity of her glare.

"I swear I've never seen you before, Soulie," he said. "At least not as a corpse."

"She would have been a young girl," Sellie told him. "She wouldn't look like this, like an ethereal being."

"There's so many. I can't be expected to wemember everybody." Death looked miffed. "That's why I keep wecords," he muttered.

"What happened to Loa at the hospital?" Soul Selector was anxious. She remembered how the connection had ripped through her and she was certain Loa had felt the agony of it, too.

"I have no idea," Death said. "I told you, soul mates are not my department. As far as I am concerned they move in mysterious ways, usually slippery."

Soul Selector turned to her scrying pool. Maybe she could locate Loa in the waters.

"But I can tell you," Death said, "that she died."

"What?" Soul Selector and Sellie both spoke at the same time.

"Loa died," he repeated. "She had a cardiac incident. She must be up here somewhere. On the Fields, like Jesse when she died with absolutely no warning. My schedule is in tatters, by the way, but nobody's asking about that."

Soul Selector started to slump, but Sellie grabbed her by the elbow. "Faint later," she said. "We need to find her."

"I'm not going back to the Titan marshes," Death said.

"We've no idea where she could be." Soul Selector's voice shook. "This place is enormous. She could be anywhere." Her nerves were shattered. She still hadn't recovered from the bone chilling torture of Loa walking right through her. It had flattened her and apparently killed the soul mate. Her soul mate.

"We need Eros," Sellie said.

"Ewos?"

"He was spying on the whole thing from the Valentine card. We need to know what he knows."

"And how the hell are we going to get him to drop by, eh?" Soul Selector knew it wasn't helpful, but she couldn't calm down and be rational. She was angry and she wanted someone else to suffer alongside her. "I know! Why don't you propose? Then we can buy an engagement card with little hearts, and arrows, and *him* sitting on it."

"I know where he will be." Sellie ignored her outburst. "He comes by the pit of shame every few days to hurl rocks. He's due about now."

"I can see how that might be fun."

Again, Sellie ignored her, but Soul Selector got the feeling it was becoming more and more difficult.

"We can set up an ambush," Sellie said.

Death clapped his hands in delight. "I've never been in an ambush," he said. Then thought a minute. "Actually, I've come along after a lot of them, but I've never actually took part. You're right, Soulie. It will be fun."

CHAPTER THIRTY-EIGHT

"What fun." Zeus looked down upon Jesse. "I didn't expect to see you again. At least, not so soon."

"Guess I missed you, Pops." The sharp gleam in his eyes told Jesse the old boy was more switched on than she'd at first thought. The wind swirled around her, lifting her hair and blowing cold air down the back of her neck. She suppressed a shiver.

"And you missed me why?" he said. "Humans always have an ulterior motive. As we say up here, there's no such thing as a free prayer."

"No such thing as a promise either, apparently." Now the gleam in his eye hardened. Jesse hoped it was for the right reason. "You gave me seven days. I barely got seven hours before Aphrodite scammed me."

"And you can prove this?"

"Death and Soul Selector were there. You need to talk to them. I'm here to lodge a complaint, but I'm damned if I'm going to sit with your nymphs for a hundred years and write it up. So this is it," she said. "This is my complaint and I'm delivering it direct. This place sucks. Your Elysian Fields are boring, your temples are freezing, your nymphs are overworked and disgruntled, you've lost your religion, you've lost touch, you cheat even on your own rules. You are all dinosaurs, but unlike the dinosaurs, you guys won't lie down and die."

She'd said it. Now she waited for true oblivion. Aphrodite had wrecked her hopes of a life, any life anywhere, with Norrie, but she'd be damned if the goddess was going to be the one to destroy her. If she was going to be stardust then the great god himself could blow her into smithereens.

"Quite the trade unionist, aren't you?" Zeus said. "I better get you out of here before you sign up the nymphs. Kronos help us all if you unionize the harpies."

Jesse had to squint hard at him before she realized he was joking.

"What do you want me to do?" he asked.

"Put me in a coma," she said.

He squinted at her. "Now that *is* an unexpected prayer."

Death took them back to the heights of Olympus. The wind howled and tore at their cloaks, while the massive ravens that circled the mountaintop screamed in anger at their intrusion.

Sellie knew of a back way into her landscape of torture that did not use the maze entrance from Zeus's great hall. She quickly bundled them into the lurid desert world of tangerine skies and lime green rock. Her sad little trench lay open before them like an empty grave.

"I can't believe I sat in there for so long," she said.

"Self-pity is a wonderful thing," Soul Selector said, while Death tsked and rubbed Sellie reassuringly on the back.

"You lost faith in yourself," he said kindly. "Self-confidence is so important. I struggle with it every day." His hand rested on her skinny shoulders.

Soul Selector rolled her eyes and gave Death a shove hard enough to propel him forward so that he, in turn, shoved Sellie back into the hole.

"Good job there, Curtains. Are we all in place?" Soul Selector edged behind a large rock. "I'll be over here. Shout when you need help."

Death found his own hiding place and they settled into their ambush positions. Soft time moved quickly, and soon they heard the swish of wings. Eros appeared overhead. He was awkward in the sky. The bulk of his body completely outweighed the tiny white wings that adorned his back and somehow kept him airborne. He landed with a thump. Shaking the lime green dust off his feet, he plodded over to Sellie's pit of shame.

"Hey, ugly!" he called and lifted a rock. "Turn around, loser, and I'll pretty you up." He raised his arm to throw.

Sellie's hand appeared over the rim of the hole and caught him by the ankle. He yelled in surprise. With a yank, she pulled him off balance down in beside her. It wasn't a deep hole so when Soul Selector and Death ran over they could clearly see Sellie pounding Eros so hard feathers flew into the air. Soul Selector reached in and dragged him out by his golden curls. His angry yells continued until he noticed he was surrounded, then with a snap of his mouth he shut up as an innate sense of self-preservation kicked in.

"My mom's gonna kill you," he blurted.

"Shut up, you little punk." Sellie slapped him and he fell quiet from shock more than obedience. "Where's the soul mate?"

"Fuck you," he said. Sellie ripped the quiver from his back. "Hey!" he shouted. "Not cool."

"I'll ask again, and then I'll begin to really hurt you. Where is the soul mate?"

"I don't know what you bitches are talking about."

"We know you were spying on us, so spill," Soul Selector said.

"My mom will—" Eros began. Sellie pulled an arrow from the quiver and he shut up at once. She examined it casually. He watched her wordlessly, his gaze glued to the arrow. She held it up to site the line of the shaft by eye.

"This is bent," she said.

"No, it's not." Eros was angry at the criticism.

"It's bent. How's target practice? Been missing much lately?" She flicked the arrow, and Eros went into spasm. "And look at the state of this fletching." She tugged on the feathered flight. He squealed and a few of his wing feathers fluttered to his feet.

"Dear me," Sellie said. "Are you somehow physically connected to these arrows? You mean to say these are not only silly little toys but, in fact, the physical embodiment of your divine powers? Do I need to be careful with these?" she asked, then whacked him on the nose with his own arrow. He cried out and covered his face with his hands.

"Not the nose, Sellie!" Death cried louder than Eros.

"I can't break it," Sellie reassured him. "Not unless I do this." She snapped the arrow in half and blood dribbled from between Eros's fingers. Death sagged against Soul Selector who was watching it all avidly. She'd found a new admiration for Sellie. She brushed Death off and he slumped against a rock.

"One more time," Sellie asked him, ignoring the tears, blood, and snot seeping between his hands from his bloodied nose. "Where is Loa?"

CHAPTER THIRTY-NINE

Sellie snapped another arrow, and the boy god squealed as if she'd snapped a rib.

"Loa?" Sellie said with a snarl. "Where is she?"

Soul Selector took a half step back. This mad, bad, dangerous to know Sellie was a little alarming. Death slipped in behind her. She knew he couldn't handle violence any more than he could sex. He was a soft soul. He might be death, but he sure as hell wasn't violence.

"Mom has her." Eros capitulated. He tenderly prodded his swollen nose. He was healing quickly though his face was still scarlet and sullen. The peachy down on his cheeks showed up against the red. The facial hair he longed for would never grow in. His divine status had left him dangling on the cusp of manhood, forever frozen as an awkward, angry, pubescent teenager.

"If she harms one hair on her head..." Soul Selector left the threat open-ended, but at the same time wondered why she bothered. There was nothing she could do against Aphrodite, no matter how the goddess behaved.

"She won't." Eros spoke back with contempt. "The new soul is too useful."

"What does she need her for?" Soul Selector asked. She tried to hide her anxiety, but it spilled over and Eros sneered at her.

"Like I'd tell you."

"You will," Sellie said, "and the sooner you start the sooner I stop doing this." She gave the quiver a hard rattle. Eros went white and his little wings wrapped around his shoulders protectively. Sellie picked out an arrow at random and flexed it between her hands. Sweat beaded on his upper lip.

"You can't do that," he whined. "I'll tell Zeus."

"Really?" Sellie released the tension on the arrow with a ping. The shaft wobbled. Eros yelled and grabbed at his crotch. "You tell Zeus and he'll come looking and what will Mama do then?"

She flexed the arrow back into an arc and released it. Eros doubled over, both hands on his dick.

"Oh, my," Sellie said. "Does this thin, willowy little arrow represent your prick? Oh, I get it. And your prick equates to an arrow of love. It's a metaphor, isn't it? Subtle." He ignored the sarcasm, preferring to whimper over his crotch. Sellie sighed. "Eros, you better prove to us that Loa's all right or I'll hand this entire quiver of arrows over to my friend here." She indicated Soul Selector. "And let her whip it against a rock for all eternity."

"And then I'll pluck you like a chicken," Soul Selector snarled, eyeing his silly little wings.

"I can't," he cried. "I don't know how to prove it." Tears shone in his eyes. He was doing his best to man up and not let the tears spill over. His wings fluttered gently around him, hugging him in tighter. Soul Selector realized they were sentient things, and seemed to care for him more than either of his parents did.

"But you're Ewos," Death said with compassion

"So?" he snarled back. Even with his dick in his hands, he hadn't the sense to behave.

"Manners," Sellie warned him. She shook the quiver and he fell to his knees with a yelp.

"You can see into dweams," Death continued, ignoring Eros's rudeness. He turned to Soul Selector and Sellie. "Because

Loa is a lover, or at least looking for love, Ewos should be able to see her dweams and at least we'd know she was okay. Wouldn't we?" He was beginning to look unconvinced at his own idea.

Sellie broke into a wide smile. "Genius. The boy's a genius." Death puffed up like a peacock. She turned to Eros. "Do it. The dream thing. Now."

He sniffed and tried to wipe away a tear so no one would notice. Soul Selector toed him in the side.

"Hurry up," she said, a growl rumbling behind her words.

He sniffed once more and said, "I need a mirror or something that reflects."

"Hold on to your feathers," she said and teleported the entire entourage to her pool with minimum effort. It was amazing what she could do when she was in a vicious mood.

"Well done," Death cooed in her ear and took up a seat on top of one of Jesse's rocks.

Sellie pointed to the pool. "Showtime, sonny."

Eros stood by the water's edge, gingerly straightening his bruised body. His hands still hovered over his tender private parts and his tiny wings shook out and resettled neatly between his shoulder blades. The pool water began to smooth out until it became flat as a mirror. Distinctive shapes began to form. A god's power far outstripped her own scrying efforts, but Soul Selector didn't care to admire Eros's skill. She wanted to see Loa. She wanted to know she was okay.

"She's in a trance," Eros said. "This is what she's dreaming of right now." He sat head lowered, barely looking at the water and huffing that he had to do anything at all.

"How do we know it's real?" Soul Selector asked, the thought suddenly occurring to her. She wouldn't trust Eros any more than she would his mother. "And not some mirage he's made up?"

"I'll know," Sellie said. "I was her soul selector. I'll recognize her dreams. I put most of them there in the first place for her to fall in love with you." She stood ramrod straight on the opposite side of the pool, her mouth a grim line in a dispassionate face.

The water cleared and a temple came into focus. The walls were high and made of stone and shone coldly in the early dawn. There was a small sacrificial pool cleaved out of the volcanic rock and rimmed in the same marble as the columns on either side. A tangle of cloth lay draped beside it. Loa entered, and the room and its details faded away and the focus centered on the pool. Except this wasn't truly Loa. It was her essence, her identity. Her sense of self felt all different in the dream. She was somehow diminished, a small unassuming soul, and Soul Selector realized she was a young girl and not the thirty-something woman who had walked right through her at the hospital that very night. The girl scanned the pool in the half light. Something wasn't right. She was worried. Her gaze slid over the bundle by the pool, then returned to it with alarm. She ran toward it and unfolded the cloth to find the body of a girl face down by the water. Loa fell to her knees and struggled to turn her over.

"Kleio," she was calling over and over, "Kleio." Bloody water soaked her white toga, and Kleio fell back onto her. Her face was a chalky mask framed by dark matted hair.

"Kleio." That last small whisper was the precursor for all the pain that was to follow. Soul Selector and Sellie winced. They knew the entirety of it. The horror of a soul essentially ripped apart but still living. They could feel the pitiless wound tearing out a hollow in the heart. A dreadful sense of failure washed over them. They had failed Loa's soul on so many levels over so many lifetimes.

Loa's tears fell on her dead love's face. The dark eyes sprung open and Kleio, suddenly and joyously alive in this fantasy of a dream, looked up at her and whispered, "Eris."

❖

The water rippled and the dreamscape fell away.

"That's all there is," Eros said, avoiding their eyes.

"I believe him," Sellie said.

"How could you let that happen?" Soul Selector shouted.

"I didn't see it," Sellie answered. "The pool didn't show me any of it. And I think you know why. Aphrodite tampered with the pool, didn't she?" she said to Eros.

He reddened but remained tight-lipped.

"Like mother, like son," she said, and cast her hand over him. "I'm done with you." He dematerialized immediately.

"Where'd he go?" Death asked, mildly alarmed.

"He's in the pit of shame," Sellie said. "He needs to spend some time in there and reflect on his behavior." The pool shimmered for an instant. Enough time for them to see Eros lying in Sellie's old pit, all his arrows encircling him in a makeshift jail. "He'll have to break those to get out. If he has the balls."

"If he breaks the wrong arrow he may not," Death pointed out.

Sellie stood with Soul Selector anxiously monitoring her face. "Are you okay?" she asked.

"I still don't understand everything," Soul Selector said.

"That was Loa's dream. A recurring one that's plagued her all her lifetimes. The one where she wakes up crying," Sellie said.

"So sad." Death mopped his tears with a monogrammed handkerchief.

"Kleio died and her soul was never resurrected," Sellie said. "She was never reunited with Eris."

"How can you be sure?" Soul Selector asked.

Sellie looked at her. "Because you are Kleio."

CHAPTER FORTY

Aphrodite's temple was as welcoming as ever. The wind blew, the columns moaned, the floor lurched, and Soul Selector's stomach lurched along with it. She'd always hated this place, and now that Loa was ensconced somewhere within it, she hated it more than ever.

"Don't lose your temper," Sellie advised her for the umpteenth time, bringing her even closer to losing her temper. She ground her teeth instead and wondered when Sellie had assumed command.

"Let's go," Sellie said. They moved out from the huddle they'd made by the entrance and strode into the main hall.

"My knees are knocking," Death mumbled. "And those swans are looking at me funny."

"Maybe your knees are annoying them," Soul Selector said. "Try taking bigger strides." She stalked on ahead leaving him to catch up.

Thalia scuttled toward them. Soul Selector was surprised to see her there. The nymph usually worked for Zeus. Maybe she freelanced? Thalia took one look at the scowling faces on the impromptu visitors and went shooting off to find Aphrodite.

"We're on the radar," Sellie muttered. They took up position before the empty throne, looking anything but worshipful.

Thalia returned. She was flustered and unhappy, but she came right up to them and said, "The goddess is not attending the temple today."

"Is she attending her manna store?" Sellie asked. Thalia blinked owlishly at her then retreated toward the rear of the throne where the manna store was hidden.

"What the hell do you think you're doing?" Aphrodite's voice came from directly behind them and made them all jump. "There is no manna store," she hissed when they faced her. "If I ever hear you speak of it again I'll have the harpies eat your tongues. Got that?"

"We want Loa." Soul Selector stepped forward. "I'm her soul selector and I want her back now." It wasn't really a lie. She was the soul selector now and she had more claim on Loa's soul than Sellie did.

"Loa?" Aphrodite looked genuinely lost for a moment, then a hard, nasty light came into her eyes. "Ah. The little soul mate. Why do you want her?"

"Because I'm her selector," Soul Selector said in disbelief. What was Aphrodite playing at? Soul mates were the soul selector's province alone. The goddess should automatically hand a soul mate over.

"You don't look after them very well, do you? This is the second one you've lost. Where is that other one, by the way, the one you were to bring me ages ago? Don't tell me you've mislaid her again?"

"Give her back!" Soul Selector roared. Death and Sellie froze in shock. The handmaidens recoiled and the entire temple hushed. This was sacrilege. No one shouted at Aphrodite. Only her voice could be raised within these walls.

The goddess paled. With a hiss, she raised her right arm to cast a thunderbolt or lightning rod or some other form of annihilation. Soul Selector squared her shoulders, ready for the blast. Behind her she could hear Death squeaking, then a mighty voice boomed out. Mighty enough to drown out the wind, mighty enough to make the marble columns quiver.

"Aphrodite, my child. What is happening here?"

Aphrodite froze. Every gaze turned toward the water fountain where a huge cob swan was swinging his snow-white wings back and forth in frantic motion. As they swept through the air, feathers danced skyward and the animal elongated by many feet to metamorphose into Zeus.

"Daddy," Aphrodite screamed, then she stamped her foot petulantly. "I always fall for the swan trick." He laughed and came forward to join them.

"How long have you been there?" she asked, the upset in her voice barely hidden.

"Not long, daughter," he said. "But enough." It was a warning, and her temper fizzled out almost at once.

"Why are you here, Daddy?" she asked, so treacly Soul Selector thought she heard flies.

"The soul mate Jesse lodged a complaint," he said.

"She what?" Aphrodite and Soul Selector both spoke at once.

"I knew I liked that girl." Zeus sounded delighted with the distraction she had provided. "She got the measure of you two all right. She knows how to work the rules around here."

"What did she do?" Sellie asked.

Zeus waved his hand in a lazy circle and the air froze into a glassy swirl. The mirrored surface continued to spin idly in mid air.

"The trick with soul mates," he said, "is to get them together quickly. Once you accomplish that, they are capable of doing everything else all by themselves."

Soul Selector and Sellie simmered with annoyance at the hyperbole. Death looked fascinated, though Soul Selector could tell it was fake.

"Jesse came to me asking to be put into a coma," Zeus continued. "How strange, I thought. Surely it can't be that boring here?" He paused, waiting for appreciation for his joke. Death tittered like a nervous chinchilla. Soul Selector and Sellie stood by sour-faced.

Zeus sniffed and continued. "It seemed she had a brilliant plan. She was going to replace a comatose soul that was due for earthly exit with her own soul. This would give her a few extra hours to connect with her earthbound soul mate who was friendly with the…coma person."

"Can you believe this?" Soul Selector muttered out the side of her mouth.

"That he's about to steal credit for our idea? Yeah," Sellie muttered back.

"I approved!" he boomed. "I sent Jesse into the empty vessel and arranged for her soul mate to visit her. It was as simple as that." He looked unbearably smug. "Why, I might even take up this soul selecting malarkey myself!" He fixed Soul Selector and Sellie with a beady eye, enjoying watching them squirm.

Death broke into hysterical laughter. Zeus beamed approval at him. "Watch and learn," he said, and the swirling mirror stopped spinning to reflect a sunny afternoon in a small hospital ward.

CHAPTER FORTY-ONE

Norrie sat by a bed in the ICU. She couldn't concentrate on her book and instead looked out the window. In the tree opposite, two collared doves were building a nest. She watched their coming and going all afternoon between cups of tea and a short chat with Rose when she came on duty. She had been lucky. If the charge nurse hadn't represented her, she wouldn't be in here at all, but as JC had no family, she was allowed to visit.

This was the second day she had called in, and still JC remained unconscious. Norrie was compelled to see her regain consciousness. She wanted to welcome JC back and perhaps tell her something of the journey that led to her return. If she was allowed to, of course. Rose had warned her to be careful. She could feel Rose's growing concern each time Norrie showed up on her floor, but she let her visit all the same. It was the only way Norrie could deal with the events of last week.

Grief was a funny thing. Norrie had spent much of her late teens in counseling for a depression that had come upon her in her sixteenth year. She had followed that up with several years of therapy as bouts of illness came and went. This had decreased as her management of her symptoms progressed. She had always believed grief to be akin to that first raw debilitation. Grief fit better than any medical model her physicians and psychiatrists could provide. She had always imagined her illness was more suited to a long-term grieving than any uni- or bipolar state. Loss was undoubtedly a catalyst to some disorders, but what had she ever lost? Loa?

She had admired Loa as a person and adored her as a lover. But a short-term lover. Loa was never going to be her one and only. And now Loa was gone and Norrie missed her terribly. But she could rationalize that loss. It was not Loa's death that crippled her. She'd known this agony much longer than she'd known Loa. What then? Her family was intact. Her career still golden. She had no addictions. Her love life stank, and her sex life was a bouquet of roses. And yet her emptiness was gargantuan. Her question was what was this emptiness? Why was she hollow?

A dry cough pulled her attention away from the doves and brought her thoughts back into the room. The figure in the bed was twitching, trying feebly to move her hands. Norrie leaped to her feet. JC was coming around. She called for Rose and was happy to disappear to the cafeteria as the medical staff did whatever they needed to. Excitement bubbled up in her as she blew on her scalding coffee and waited to see if she'd be allowed to return to the side ward.

Rose let her visit but cautioned it could only be for a minute. JC was doing well but was exhausted. Her consultant was delighted with her, though. "We'll give her an hour or two then we're moving her to post-op. It's just across the hall."

JC was propped up in bed at a slight incline. Her ventilator tube had gone and she was breathing by herself, though many other tubes and drains still ran in and out under the bedclothes. She gave a tired, wobbly smile as Norrie entered.

"Hi. I'm Norrie," she said. "I'm a friend."

"More water, please?" JC's voice was raw and underused. She weakly indicated the lipped drinking cup on the bedside table.

"Here." Gently, Norrie held the cup to her lips and watched JC sip.

"I'm Jesse," JC finally whispered when she'd had enough water.

"JC," Norrie gently corrected her. "You're JC."

JC frowned at this. "I am?" She seemed confused. Norrie nodded.

"Do I know you?" she asked next, though it obviously hurt to talk. "I feel like I know you."

"Sh," Norrie said. "We have all the time in the world to talk later. Right now you need to rest."

"Feel like I've been out of it forever." JC's eyes began to shut. "Don't go," she murmured, reaching out for Norrie's hand before falling into an exhausted sleep.

"I won't." Norrie made her promise to JC's pale, worn out face. "I'll be here for you. I'll look after you. I promise." She kissed the thin white knuckles she held in her own warm hands, as if to seal the promise. "You're safe now."

❖

"It's so beautiful," Death cooed. "I love a happy ending."

"What's she doing going to post-op?" Sellie asked, always the pragmatist.

"Yes," Soul Selector said. "How can she be post-op when she hasn't had an operation?"

They looked at Zeus in askance and the smug look slid off his face. He had no idea what was going on outside of Jesse's remit. The godhead couldn't think on his feet, and Soul Selector was delighted. *That'll put him back in his box. Big fat know-it-all.*

"Did you really think your half-formed plan would work?" Aphrodite finally spoke up, stating what everyone was thinking. But then Zeus was her father and not likely to flatten her insolence with lightning. "Look, people, I need manna and I need soul mates to make it. Loa and Norrie were never going to work as a couple. Nothing I could do could make them fall in love. In lust, yes, no problem, they were young, healthy women after all. But fall in love? No. That wasn't going to happen."

"I knew it!" Soul Selector pointed at her. "I knew you had that little toad fire arrows at them."

"You watch who you're calling a toad. He's my baby!"

"Children, children." Zeus tried to stop the argument with good, sporting humor. "I understand my grandson is hale and hearty and in a hole. Is that right, soul selector?" Soul Selector noted he asked Sellie rather than her. *So, he's known about the pit of shame all along and he let Aphrodite get away with it. And he let Sellie sit in it for thousands of years in total misery.*

"Why not? He seemed to like that particular hole." Sellie's tone was cold. "He was always hovering around it."

Aphrodite glared at her through slitted eyes, and Soul Selector had to admire the way Sellie straightened her back and glared right back. Zeus looked about as happy as a man who had stepped in a big puddle of PMS. He shifted uncomfortably and began glancing sideways for the exit.

"About this operation JC had," he asked, "is it really pertinent? Surely we can call a close to this episode now?"

"What did you do to her?" Soul Selector stood inches from Aphrodite. She trembled with suppressed anger. Sellie came to stand shoulder to shoulder with her. Soul mates were their jurisdiction and no place for gods to be meddling. Not even the higher Pantheon could touch their charges.

"I gave her a few extra hours in her coma." Aphrodite was becoming bored. Any minute now, she would blow them all off and disappear, tired of all the questions and certain she could pacify Zeus later. "If I could get Jesse and that other girl to commit as soul mates, then Loa would be the odd one out. So I killed her and her organs went to JC, or Jesse, whatever.

Now she has a lovely new liver and a lovely new girlfriend, and hopefully many years to make me manna. And we don't have to wait around for reincarnation either." Her triumphant announcement was directed at Zeus. He looked surprised and pleased.

"You interfering—" Soul Selector snarled.

"Where is the Loa soul mate now?" Sellie talked over her. Loudly.

Aphrodite turned her back. Their time was up. She linked arms with Zeus and, together, the great gods glided away across the marbled temple floor until they dissolved into windblown particles and disappeared.

"Bastards," Soul Selector muttered through her teeth.

"Gods are always cheaters," Death said. "They never have to pay."

"We'll find her," Sellie told her. "She'll be somewhere in the Fields."

"She's been pushed into the queue for reincarnation." Thalia came to usher them out. She spoke softly so as not to be overheard. "She's over by the Styx as good as beyond reach. You'll have to wait for her soul to come round again."

"How do you know this?" Soul Selector whispered.

"I was there when Aphrodite decreed it. No one wants singular soul mates drifting about the Fields," she said. "They have to be put to use or dumped." Red spots appeared on Thalia's cheeks. She was angry. They came to the main doorway, and Thalia indicated they should leave.

"You'll have to wait for her reincarnation. Sorry." Her words followed them out.

"She's gone." Soul Selector was in shock.

"But she'll come back." Sellie tried to console her. "It may take a couple of hundred years, but you'll get to see her again."

"At least she's not been slushied," Death said helpfully. And that was the only blessing.

EPILOGUE

Despite fighting me every inch of the way, Jesse and Norrie are happy now. They are still on earth and deeply in love, pumping out tons of good energy into the universe, and unfortunately into Aphrodite's coffers.

I have dug Sellie a new hole. It's by my scrying pool, a place where only soul selectors go. I hope it's deep enough. I dug for ages just to make sure.

It's in the copse of jacaranda trees Jesse made, no more than a smoky dot on the horizon of the Elysian Fields. She feels safe there, and often we sit by the water and chat as the stars come out. I think we are friends, of a sort.

Loa, or rather Eris, is lost in time. She will return, eventually. Time is the tide on which we all wash up. I will wait for her. A hundred years, a thousand years; it is nothing to me. Aphrodite knows this. But what can she do but wait along with me? Despite her machinations, I am still the Soul Selector. I work for her department. I know about her manna stash. I help make that manna, that food of the gods, and I hope they choke on it.

I will not abide by their rules any longer. Their diktats bend like the reeds around my pool. They sway this way and that like the Jacaranda blossoms above my head. I have no time for their rules. Jesse was right. I was a fool to follow them. So now I will follow my heart. I will make my own rules, follow my own groove, I will own this place, and things will be done *my* way, at least until Eris returns. From this day on, I am not the Soul Selector. I am Soul Selecta.

The End

About the Author

Gill McKnight is Irish and moves between Ireland, England, and Greece in a non-stop circuit of work, rest, and play. She loves messing about in boats and has secret fantasies about lavender farming.

With a BA in Art and Design and a Masters in Art History it says much about her artistic skill that she now works in IT.

Books Available from Bold Strokes Books

Love's Bounty by Yolanda Wallace. Lobster boat captain Jake Myers stopped living the day she cheated death, but meeting greenhorn Shy Silva stirs her back to life. (978-1-62639334-9)

Just Three Words by Melissa Brayden. Sometimes the one you want is the one you least suspect. Accountant Samantha Ennis has her ordered life disrupted when heartbreaker Hunter Blair moves into her trendy Soho loft. (978-1-62639-335-6)

Lay Down the Law by Carsen Taite. Attorney Peyton Davis returns to her Texas roots to take on big oil and the Mexican Mafia, but will her investigation thwart her chance at true love? (978-1-62639-336-3)

Playing in Shadow by Lesley Davis. Survivor's guilt threatens to keep Bryce trapped in her nightmare world unless Scarlet's love can pull her out of the darkness back into the light. (978-1-62639-337-0)

Soul Selecta by Gill McKnight. Soul mates are hell to work with. (978-1-62639-338-7)

The Revelation of Beatrice Darby by Jean Copeland. Adolescence is complicated, but Beatrice Darby is about to discover how impossible it can seem to a lesbian coming of age in conservative 1950s New England. (978-1-62639-339-4)

Twice Lucky by Mardi Alexander. For firefighter Mackenzie James and Dr. Sarah Macarthur, there's suddenly a whole lot more in life to understand, to consider, to risk…someone will need to fight for her life. (978-1-62639-325-7)

Shadow Hunt by L.L. Raand. With young to raise and her Pack under attack, Sylvan, Alpha of the wolf Weres, takes on her greatest challenge when she determines to uncover the faceless enemies known as the Shadow Lords. A Midnight Hunters novel. (978-1-62639-326-4)

Heart of the Game by Rachel Spangler. A baseball writer falls for a single mom, but can she ever love anything as much as she loves the game? (978-1-62639-327-1)

Getting Lost by Michelle Grubb. Twenty-eight days, thirteen European countries, a tour manager fighting attraction, and an accused murderer: Stella and Phoebe's journey of a lifetime begins here. (978-1-62639-328-8)

Prayer of the Handmaiden by Merry Shannon. Celibate priestess Kadrian must defend the kingdom of Ithyria from a dangerous enemy and ultimately choose between her duty to the Goddess and the love of her childhood sweetheart, Erinda. (978-1-62639-329-5)

The Witch of Stalingrad by Justine Saracen. A Soviet "night witch" pilot and American journalist meet on the Eastern Front in WW II and struggle through carnage, conflicting politics, and the deadly Russian winter. (978-1-62639-330-1)

Pedal to the Metal by Jesse J. Thoma. When unreformed thief Dubs Williams is released from prison to help Max Winters bust a car theft ring, Max learns that to catch a thief, get in bed with one. (978-1-62639-239-7)

Dragon Horse War by D. Jackson Leigh. A priestess of peace and a fiery warrior must defeat a vicious uprising that entwines their destinies and ultimately their hearts. (978-1-62639-240-3)

For the Love of Cake by Erin Dutton. When everything is on the line, and one taste can break a heart, will pastry chefs Maya and Shannon take a chance on reality? (978-1-62639-241-0)

Betting on Love by Alyssa Linn Palmer. A quiet country-girl-at-heart and a live-life-to-the-fullest biker take a risk at offering each other their hearts. (978-1-62639-242-7)

The Deadening by Yvonne Heidt. The lines between good and evil, right and wrong, have always been blurry for Shade. When Raven's actions force her to choose, which side will she come out on? (978-1-62639-243-4)

Ordinary Mayhem by Victoria A. Brownworth. Faye Blakemore has been taking photographs since she was ten, but those same photographs threaten to destroy everything she knows and everything she loves. (978-1-62639-315-8)

One Last Thing by Kim Baldwin & Xenia Alexiou. Blood is thicker than pride. The final book in the Elite Operative Series brings together foes, family, and friends to start a new order. (978-1-62639-230-4)

Songs Unfinished by Holly Stratimore. Two aspiring rock stars learn that falling in love while pursuing their dreams can be harmonious—if they can only keep their pasts from throwing them out of tune. (978-1-62639-231-1)

Beyond the Ridge by L.T. Marie. Will a contractor and a horse rancher overcome their family differences and find common ground to build a life together? (978-1-62639-232-8)

Swordfish by Andrea Bramhall. Four women battle the demons from their pasts. Will they learn to let go, or will happiness be forever beyond their grasp? (978-1-62639-233-5)

The Fiend Queen by Barbara Ann Wright. Princess Katya and her consort Starbride must turn evil against evil in order to banish Fiendish power from their kingdom, and only love will pull them back from the brink. (978-1-62639-234-2)

Up the Ante by PJ Trebelhorn. When Jordan Stryker and Ashley Noble meet again fifteen years after a short-lived affair, are either of them prepared to gamble on a chance at love? (978-1-62639-237-3)

Speakeasy by MJ Williamz. When mob leader Helen Byrne sets her sights on the girlfriend of Al Capone's right-hand man, passion and tempers flare on the streets of Chicago. (978-1-62639-238-0)

Venus in Love by Tina Michele. Morgan Blake can't afford any distractions and Ainsley Dencourt can't afford to lose control—but the beauty of life and art usually lies in the unpredictable strokes of the artist's brush. (978-1-62639-220-5)

Rules of Revenge by AJ Quinn. When a lethal operative on a collision course with her past agrees to help a CIA analyst on a critical assignment, the encounter proves explosive in ways neither woman anticipated. (978-1-62639-221-2)

The Romance Vote by Ali Vali. Chili Alexander is a sought-after campaign consultant who isn't prepared when her boss's daughter, Samantha Pellegrin, comes to work at the firm and shakes up Chili's life from the first day. (978-1-62639-222-9)

Advance: Exodus Book One by Gun Brooke. Admiral Dael Caydoc's mission to find a new homeworld for the Oconodian people is hazardous, but working with the infuriating Commander Aniwyn "Spinner" Seclan endangers her heart and soul. (978-1-62639-224-3)

UnCatholic Conduct by Stevie Mikayne. Jil Kidd goes undercover to investigate fraud at St. Marguerite's Catholic School, but life gets complicated when her student is killed— and she begins to fall for her prime target. (978-1-62639-304-2)

Season's Meetings by Amy Dunne. Catherine Birch reluctantly ventures on the festive road trip from hell with beautiful stranger Holly Daniels only to discover the road to true love has its own obstacles to maneuver. (978-1-62639-227-4)

Myth and Magic: Queer Fairy Tales edited by Radclyffe and Stacia Seaman. Myth, magic, and monsters—the stuff of childhood dreams (or nightmares) and adult fantasies. (978-1-62639-225-0)

Nine Nights on the Windy Tree by Martha Miller. Recovering drug addict, Bertha Brannon, is an attorney who is trying to stay clean when a murder sends her back to the bad end of town. (978-1-62639-179-6)

Driving Lessons by Annameekee Hesik. Dive into Abbey Brooks's sophomore year as she attempts to figure out the amazing, but sometimes complicated, life of a you-know-who girl at Gila High School. (978-1-62639-228-1)

Asher's Shot by Elizabeth Wheeler. Asher Price's candid photographs capture the truth, but when his success requires exposing an enemy, Asher discovers his only shot at happiness involves revealing secrets of his own. (978-1-62639-229-8)

Courtship by Carsen Taite. Love and justice—a lethal mix or a perfect match? (978-1-62639-210-6)

Against Doctor's Orders by Radclyffe. Corporate financier Presley Worth wants to shut down Argyle Community Hospital, but Dr. Harper Rivers will fight her every step of the way, if she can also fight their growing attraction. (978-1-62639-211-3)

A Spark of Heavenly Fire by Kathleen Knowles. Kerry and Beth are building their life together, but unexpected circumstances could destroy their happiness. (978-1-62639-212-0)

Never Too Late by Julie Blair. When Dr. Jamie Hammond is forced to hire a new office manager, she's shocked to come face to face with Carla Grant and memories from her past. (978-1-62639-213-7)

Widow by Martha Miller. Judge Bertha Brannon must solve the murder of her lover, a policewoman she thought she'd grow old with. As more bodies pile up, the murderer starts coming for her. (978-1-62639-214-4)

Twisted Echoes by Sheri Lewis Wohl. What's a woman to do when she realizes the voices in her head are real? (978-1-62639-215-1)

Criminal Gold by Ann Aptaker. Through a dangerous night in New York in 1949, Cantor Gold, dapper dyke-about-town, smuggler of fine art, is forced by a crime lord to be his instrument of vengeance. (978-1-62639-216-8)

The Melody of Light by M.L. Rice. After surviving abuse and loss, will Riley Gordon be able to navigate her first year of college and accept true love and family? (978-1-62639-219-9)

Because of You by Julie Cannon. What would you do for the woman you were forced to leave behind? (978-1-62639-199-4)

The Job by Jove Belle. Sera always dreamed that she would one day reunite with Tor. She just didn't think it would involve terrorists, firearms, and hostages. (978-1-62639-200-7)

Making Time by C.J. Harte. Two women going in different directions meet after fifteen years and struggle to reconnect in spite of the past that separated them. (978-1-62639-201-4)

Once The Clouds Have Gone by KE Payne. Overwhelmed by the dark clouds of her past, Tag Grainger is lost until the intriguing and spirited Freddie Metcalfe unexpectedly forces her to reevaluate her life. (978-1-62639-202-1)